# GREEK MYTHS, WESTERN STYLE

# GREEK MYTHS, WESTERN STYLE
## TOGA TALES WITH AN ATTITUDE

Barbara McBride-Smith

August House Publishers, Inc.

LITTLE ROCK

Published 1998 by August House, Inc.,
P.O. Box 3223, Little Rock, Arkansas, 72203,
501-372-5450.


Printed in the United States of America


10 9 8 7 6 5 4 3 2 1


LIBRARY OF CONGRESS
CATALOGING-IN-PUBLICATION DATA
McBride-Smith, Barbara, 1944–
Greek myths, western style:
toga tales with an attitude / Barbara McBride-Smith.
p. cm.
Includes bibliographical references (p. 121)
ISBN 0–87483–524–0
1. Texas—Social life and customs —Fiction.
2. Mythology, Greek—Fiction. I. Title.
PS3563.C33367   G74 1998
813'.54—dc21      98–27423


Executive editor: Liz Parkhurst
Project editor: Jan Cottingham
Book design and illustration:
Patrick McKelvey and Katrina Kelso, AdManInc.


AUGUST HOUSE, INC.   PUBLISHERS   LITTLE ROCK

*For Dale*

*"Now cracks a noble heart.*
*Good night, sweet prince,*
*And flights of angels sing thee to thy rest."*

# CONTENTS

# INTRODUCTION

The stories in this book didn't spring fully grown, a la Athena, from my head. Nor did I carry them in my upper thigh, nurturing them until they were ready to be born. I didn't even have to go to Hades and back for these tales. *Au contraire*, as we say back home, I got them the easy way. I borrowed them ... from the ancient Greek tellers of tales. Homer and Hesiod and Euripides and Aristophanes would understand. They did the same thing. Just as they did, I grew up with these stories. I saw them reincarnated in Waco, Texas—where life was a lot more like a mythological soap opera than I cared to admit for a long time. It still is.

In my adolescence, when I consumed everything I could get my hands on at the public library, I discovered the works of Edith Hamilton, Robert Graves, and Thomas Bulfinch. My response was amazement and an overwhelming sense of déjà vu. "I know these people!" I proclaimed. They were the strong women, the rednecks, the jocks, the cheerleaders, and the cowboys who inhabited my hometown in the 1950s and '60s.

The names had been changed to protect the guilty, but the intrigue, the humor, and the debauchery were the same. I knew Ol' Man Zeus, a gun-totin' Big Daddy, the orneriest guy in town who had enough money and power to buy himself a political office. I recognized the Metheus brothers, Pro and Epi, high

9

school all-state football heroes who never got over their glory days. I dated Theseus, who was so dumb he couldn't drink beer out of a boot if the instructions were printed on the heel. He abandoned me at the Orpheum movie theater when he got arrested for driving with a year's backlog of speeding tickets piled ankle-deep in the floorboard of his Chevy. I recognized the sexpot Aphrodite as our own basketball queen, whose two outstanding attributes were neither athletic skill nor brains. I could point out to you Jason-the-jerk who jilted his wife after she put him through Baylor Law School (she got even, by the way), Pandora-the-debutante who got framed by the good ol' boys, and Athena-the-leader-of-the-Moral-Minority who was none other than our beloved high school girls' counselor.

Waco was hip-deep in hubris!

Edith Hamilton said—and if she didn't, she should have—that Greece was the cradle of Western civilization. How far west she meant, I wasn't sure, but I figured it must have included central Texas. Ah, the truth was sweet!

And then I grew up and went away to Boston to get educated and cultured, so that I would amount to more than a hill of beans. I tried to forget the colorful truth of my youth and my Southern drawl. It didn't work. You can take the gal out of Texas, but ... well, you know. What I did discover is that the Greek deities and heroes are alive and well everywhere you go. They may talk with a different accent or struggle with different monsters, but they are we, the universal we.

While living in the artsy and intellectual world of Harvard Square in the 1970s, I discovered a "new" performance art called storytelling. People there were actually getting paid to do something my family and neighbors back home had done for free all their lives. I concluded that storytelling might be as much a part of a Yankee's genetic makeup as it was a Southerner's.

Eventually, the fates moved me to Oklahoma, which, to a Texan, is like going to Hades' underworld. It turned out to be not nearly so deadly as my daddy had always warned me. It has been, in fact, the kindest and gentlest place I've ever lived. Here I've found my real voice as a storyteller: a middle-aged do-right woman with an incurable drawl, feminist sympathies, and a kiss-my-chicken-fried-steak attitude.

Two people who helped me work through the process of reconciling my past with my present to create the stories you see in this book were Dr. Dale Maxwell, my friend and mentor (whom I met in a community theater production when I first moved to Oklahoma), and Dr. Dennis Smith, my husband and best critic (who was my high school Apollo). The three of us, along with Dale's wife, Tana, worked as collaborators on the stories I began to tell as a freelance storyteller. Dale, a psychiatrist by profession, was Sigmund Freud, Julia Child, and Willie Nelson all rolled into one great big guy. He found a hook for every myth— psychologically speaking: what it was that made those people do all that crazy stuff. Tana Maxwell recalls how it all began:

*I awoke one Saturday morning to find Dale poised among a pile of Greek mythology books, listening to Willie Nelson on the stereo, drinking black coffee, and scribbling notes furiously on a yellow legal pad. His big blue eyes were twinkling and he was chuckling to himself. As the sun was rising over our Oklahoma home, Orpheus was born anew.*

*A couple of months later, we were visiting with our friend Barbara McBride-Smith, planning a Christmas celebration for our local community theater. Barbara, not only an actress, librarian, wife, and mother, but also at that time a budding storyteller, became really excited when Dale introduced her to his vision of Orpheus. After pondering the scribbled notes and doing some revising and tweaking, she and Dale struck a deal. She would debut Orpheus at the theater Christmas party. She said, "I'm not the classical type, but if I tell it like a good ol' girl who really knew Orpheus, do you think it might still work?" That was exactly what Dale was hoping for, so he agreed that it just might. And did it ever!*

*That event marked the beginning of many hours of discussion, disagreement, epiphany, and absolute joy as we cooked up new recipes for old myths we all loved. Dennis, Barbara's husband, joined our myth team as a valuable historical consultant. And later a wonderfully creative musician named Jed Butler came on board to help give a little rhythm and rap to our projects. We all laughed and cried together as we listened to Barbara make these stories spring to life at storytelling festivals all over the country. And for about ten years, we had more fun than the law allows.*

And then, Dale went and died on us. Cancer. He was only 56. I can still hear his voice. It's in these stories. He was a complex man—brilliant, funny, generous, cantankerous as all get-out at times, but the sweetest friend I ever had. I surely do miss him.

I promised him I'd go on telling these stories, many of which grew from the nuggets of gold he gave me. We talked during his waning months about publishing the stories, but I struggled with how they might become static once frozen in print, or how the sound and feel of live performance could never be captured on paper. "Aw, get over that hang-up," said Dale. "Homer felt the same way three thousand years ago. He probably rolled over in his grave when somebody wrote his stuff down. Write 'em the same way you tell 'em.

Anybody who's smart and has a sense of humor is bound to like 'em. You can quote me!"

So here they are, my renditions of a few ancient tales—a kaleidoscope of symbols that illuminate my own lifetime of reality. I hope you like 'em. And if they make you want to re-read Homer, Hesiod, Euripides, and those other old Greeks to see if I'm telling the truth, then I've done what I set out to do.

—*Barbara McBride-Smith, 1998*

# THE CREATION

In the beginning ... Well, let me tell it to you the way Uncle Homer would have told it, as best I can piece it together. Uncle Homer was a good ol' boy. His eyesight wasn't too sharp, but he had a memory like an elephant. Just imagine him telling you this tale while he was strumming on his banjo and chawing on a plug of Bull Durham. He'd be sitting in his rocking chair on the front porch, and everybody would be gathered around listening to him spin another one of his yarns. Here it goes:

I don't reckon anybody knows exactly *when* it all began, but trust me, it was a good while back. And whenever it was, all that there was ... was nothing. Absolutely nothing. Kind of hard to wrap your mind around, ain't it? But this nothingness had a name. It was called Chaos. Must have been a mighty big mess of nothing. And some way or another, light and dark separated from Chaos, and that caused a spark of friction. And from that spark erupted a beautiful creature called Mama Earth. Mama Earth called herself Gaea.

Gaea, Mama Earth, was beautiful and lush and fertile. She looked around at the nothingness and the light and the dark, and she said, "I'm lonely. I'll make me a man!" So she did. She gave birth to him all by herself. Yeah, I know what you're thinking: that's impossible! Hey, just go with me on this, OK? It's called parthenogenesis, and this wasn't the only time in history it ever happened.

Now this husband that Mama Earth birthed for herself was Father Sky. She called him Uranus, or Uri for short. Uri was a real romantic at first. He covered Mama Earth like a warm blanket, and he showered her with hugs and kisses. The showers seeped down into her nooks and crannies, and by spring Mama Earth was great big with child. Children, actually. Fact is, she gave birth to three litters in all.

In her first litter were three boys. The ugliest three fellers you ever saw. Each one of 'em had fifty heads and one hundred hands. See, that's what comes of marrying your relatives. No sooner were those Hecatonchires—that's what Mama Earth called those boys— no sooner were they weaned than she birthed her second litter. She had three more boys this time, and they were nearly as ugly as the first three. They each had one big ol' eye, instead of two, right in the middle of their forehead. Mama Earth was proud of her kids, though. She called that second bunch Cyclopes. Their daddy Uri was downright disgusted with his own offspring, or maybe he was just irritated that Mama Earth was paying more attention to them than to him. So Uri grabbed those six ugly younguns, carried 'em off, and chained 'em up in a dark cave. Well, he and Mama Earth nearly split the sheet over that.

Before long, though, Uri used his warm-blanket-and-shower-of-love routine on Mama Earth, and she let him back into her good graces. For a while. Her third litter was an even dozen. Six beautiful girls and six handsome boys. They were huge. They were gigantic. They were titanic. So Mama Earth called them Titans. "Oh, these babies are unsinkable," she thought.

But Uri began to grow jealous of his twelve lovely Titan kids, and he made secret plans to lock 'em away in the cave with their six ugly brothers. Mama Earth told her oldest Titan boy, Cronus, it was time for him to take his daddy down a notch or two. She made that boy a weapon with a very sharp blade. It was called a sickle. Well, what happened next wasn't pretty. Young Cronus became the Grim Reaper. He took away his daddy's manhood. Literally.

Now Cronus was the *número uno* in the family (except for his mama Gaea, of course) and Cronus needed a wife. Seeing as how his pickings were sort of slim, he chose Rhea, one of his sisters. They had a Titanic wedding, and then began to produce their own family.

Their first baby was pretty enough to be a goddess. They named her Hestia, and were so proud of her perfect little fingers and toes. But before long, Cronus began to worry. What if his kids did to him what he had done to his daddy? The very idea was real painful to Cronus. He couldn't take any chances, so he swallowed his own baby daughter. Gulped her right down and figured he had solved his problems. Rhea gave birth to four more children—Demeter, Hera, Hades, and Poseidon—and Cronus consumed each one. Chug-a-lugged them without even

17

asking their names. He was feeling downright cocky, having his cake and eating it too.

When their sixth youngun was born, a strong little feller named Zeus, Rhea hid him on an island before Cronus could hear the baby cry. Then Rhea wrapped a big ol' rock in a baby blanket, showed it to Cronus, and he gulped down that rock without even taking a good look at it.

Meanwhile, little Zeus grew up on that island. He drank goat's milk and ate wild honey and ran with the coyotes. When he got to be a big strapping adolescent, his mama decided it was time to bring him home. Obviously, she hadn't had any previous experience with adolescents, or she might have been inclined to leave him out there on that island a few more years. But as luck would have it, Zeus and his mama Rhea got along fine and dandy. She gave him a job in the kitchen, serving beverages and snacks to his daddy. Rhea told Cronus this new hired hand was a distant nephew, not worth spit for doing much else. Cronus bought it—hook, line, and sinker.

While Cronus was sitting around on his fat laurels, Rhea and Zeus were plotting against the old man. Rhea knew this recipe for an emetic—an upchuck potion, in other words. Try it sometime. Mix up some mustard and warm water and take a swig. Guaranteed to make you toss your cookies! Rhea stirred that nasty stuff into Cronus's good dark ale, and Zeus served it to him.

Sure enough, Cronus started hurling everything he had ever eaten. Up came his five kids, and they hit the ground running. They headed for that cave where their six ugly uncles, the

Hecatonchires and the Cyclopes, were chained up. The kids released the ugly uncles and they all came after Cronus, loaded for bear. Well, the fight was on. And when the dust settled, Cronus was the big-time loser, and Zeus was king of the hill. Literally.

Rhea's six younguns—Zeus and Hestia and Hera and Demeter and Hades and Poseidon—settled down on a gorgeous piece of real estate up in the hill country given to them by their grandma, Gaea. They became the first generation of Olympian gods. As time went by, they had a whole bunch of kids and grandkids of their own. They even invented human beings and got into all sorts of other trouble. They're a wild bunch, but a lot of fun when you get to know 'em. Last I heard, they're all still alive and doing right well up yonder on Olympus.

And that's the story of how it all began.

# ORPHEUS

Orpheus was a picker. Not your everyday picker. He was Tom T., Jerry Lee, Willie, and Chet all rolled into one. Some folks say his mama had an "in" with the muses. I reckon that's true, because Orpheus had rhythm and blues genes like nobody had ever had before.

Back when Orpheus was just getting started, he signed on to play for Jason for a while. You remember Jason. Everybody called him "the old fleece-chaser." His bus was a boat called the Argo, and he hired Orpheus to play for his crew. Orpheus could count cadence with his guitar better than any Ivy League rowing team's coxswain could yell it. He would play for those Argonauts when they were dog-tired but needed to make a few extra miles in a day. He'd also play for them when they were on R&R. His sweet notes would massage their sore muscles and make those boys forget all about their pain.

Well, one day Orpheus really saved their bacon. There was this rock group called the Sirens. Those gals could draw a crowd like the Beatles and Elvis Presley on a twin bill. If they'd had a better location, they would have busted all attendance records. You've heard about folks getting trampled at rock concerts? Well, I tell you what, it was worse than that where the Sirens played.

So one day, the Argo was floating along, nobody in any particular hurry, when the sound of the Sirens came across the waves. Talk about a strong repetitive hook—those gals had it! The Argonauts started rowing that boat a little faster, heading right toward the Sirens. They wanted to get up real close for a better listen. But Orpheus knew trouble when he heard it. Those gals had a habit of bumping folks down a notch or two on the food chain, if you know what I mean. Orpheus started picking out some fancy cadence licks of his own and overrode the fancy sound system of the Sirens. He got the crew out of earshot just in the nick of time. If it hadn't been for Orpheus, that would've been the last curtain call for Jason and the Argonauts.

But the story that folks really like to tell about Orpheus isn't so much about his picking as it is about his flat-out bad-luck love life. His lady was a sweet thing named Eurydice. Nobody had ever heard of her until Orpheus started running around with her. Everybody did notice, however, that after he met her his music got even better than usual. It was no surprise when they decided to get hitched up. The wedding was a big deal. It was one of those outdoor shindigs with enough brew and barbecue to put L.B.J. to shame. After they had finished the ceremony and everybody had started to party down, Eurydice went for a walk through the meadow with her bridesmaids. She was giving them some encouragement about their prospects and all when ... when a viper up and bit her! Married five minutes and bit by a snake!

Orpheus didn't seem to care about his music after Eurydice died. He sat around on rocks and smoked more and drank more and slept less. He couldn't find his ego with both hands. He missed her a bunch, and he got mad because he said it just wasn't fair. Everybody thinks, when they're young, that life is supposed to be fair. They find out, when they get older, that it never is. Now Orpheus could have stayed depressed, and pretty soon everybody would have forgotten all about him. But he decided to do something about his situation, and that's why lots of folks have heard of him today.

He set out with nothing but his guitar. No ax, no hammer, no bow and arrow. That wasn't his style. He was going on a long journey. He was going down to see the Man, the one some folks call Hades. It's not easy to get through to the Man. It was gonna take some powerful picking to pull this off. He traveled down, down, down a long way. He came to this place called the Styx— and it was.

This next part sounds a little hokey, but it's true. There was this three-headed dog guarding the entrance. Honest, three heads! And this pup had been keeping everybody that didn't belong there away from that door for a long time. He was one mean mutt. Well, Orpheus started picking out a tune. I don't know for sure what song it was. But I like to think that maybe he finger-picked all four parts to an Oak Ridge Boys tune and those three dog heads went crazy trying to go from four-part to three-part harmony without losing any notes. Probably the truth is, it was just some simple ditty, but the sound came through so clear and clean it completely filled up those dog heads with music till there wasn't room left for any snarl in them.

So Orpheus finally did get in to see the Man. They sat down in a big cave with fires burning all around. Orpheus strummed a little, mellowing things out, while he talked real nice to the Man. He said he didn't want anything that belonged to the Man. The Man was going to get Eurydice one of these days anyway. Orpheus said he just wanted to borrow her for a while. He wanted his fair share of time with her up on the earth. Besides, what was time to the Man? While he was talking about how life ought to be fair, he was strumming the whole time. One thing he said still sticks in my mind. He said: "The bud was plucked before the flower bloomed." Now that's pure poetry. If that boy had had half the interest in writing lyrics that he had in picking, we'd all still be singing his songs today. But he wasn't interested in writing words at all. What he did best was take anybody's average song and fill it up with his sweet music so that it sounded like the Boston Pops playing and the Mormon Tabernacle Choir singing—all at once!

Well, whaddya know, the Man bought it. Guess he doesn't get much soothing music down there. He was in the best mood he'd been in for a mighty long time. He said that Orpheus could take Eurydice back on home with him. But there was one little condition. Orpheus couldn't look back to see if Eurydice was following him until both of them were clean out of the Man's territory. After all he'd been through, and poor Orpheus couldn't even get a peek at her. The truth is, she didn't look so good, having been dead all that time. She wouldn't be herself again until she breathed some good clean air. But Orpheus was just itching to lay eyes on her. So he started out of there, hoping she was behind him, hoping she was keeping up. He didn't know if he could stand it until he got back up to the light of day. Well, he made it! Sort of. He pulled up out of that hole in the ground, just busting to see her, and he spun around. I don't know what happened exactly. She must have stumbled climbing out, or maybe her heel got caught in her dress, but she wasn't all the way out of the ground when Orpheus looked back at her. He got one glimpse of her ... and she just ... disappeared. Orpheus knew it was over. If you mess up, you can't go begging to the Man again. Eurydice was gone, and she wasn't ever coming back.

Orpheus never amounted to anything after that. He played his music, but his heart wasn't in it. He didn't associate with any of the good people he knew. He just didn't give a rip anymore. His gigs got rougher and rougher, and one day a bunch of mean biker-types just flat-out tore him up. The folks that loved him and remembered his music gathered up the pieces of him they could find. They buried Orpheus deep in the heart of Texas—Austin, I believe. And some folks say that's why to this day the music is a little sweeter down that way.

# DEMETER AND PERSEPHONE

A long time ago, the earth was lush and fertile. I mean *green*—every day was Saint Patrick's Day—that kind of green. And the crops? They grew all year round. If you think you have a hard time now giving away your extra zucchini and tomatoes, you ought to be glad you didn't live back in those days.

Then, one day—nobody knew why—the green turned yellow. And the yellow turned brown. The ground grew colder and colder and harder and harder. You could water and you could fertilize and you could stand on your head and chant under a full moon at midnight, but the ground was putting out zip.

Down the road from us apiece there lived this right attractive yellow-haired lady named Demeter. She knew more about farming than a frog knows about being watertight. So I decided to take a walk down there and see if she knew what was happening.

I'll never forget the moment I first saw her. There she was sitting on an old tree stump, with a look on her face that said,

"Don't mess with me!" She appeared to be a woman who'd been rode hard and put up wet. When a woman looks like that, you'd best leave her alone.

I was about to turn around and tiptoe back up the road, but she spotted me and gave me a glare that stopped me dead in my tracks. Then her face relaxed just a bit, and she motioned for me to come on over and sit down with her on that tree stump. I was willing to do anything that would make her happy, so I took a seat.

We sat there a good while, saying nothing. She commenced to staring out over the fields again. Then she said, "You see these fields? Have you ever seen any farmland drier than this? Of course you haven't. But it's gonna get drier than this. Even a lizard won't be able to survive. And it's not just these fields here. You can walk in any direction as far as you want, and it's gonna be the same story. Dried-up fields, withered crops, drought and famine, cold and misery. Honey, I'm telling you these fields ain't never gonna grow anything again. That'll teach him to mess with me!"

As she spoke, she began to look up toward the big house on the hill. It was a huge, sprawling plantation house, with the white columns in front, magnolia trees in the back, and crape myrtles growing along the walk. Looked sort of like a palace. It was owned by the richest, most powerful man in these parts. Everybody called him Old Zeus. Of all the big cheeses around, he was the biggest. Folks got a little shaky when they talked about him. He wasn't always mean. He could be real generous ... sometimes. But he did expect to get his way about everything. Folks said if you rubbed him the wrong way and got on his bad side, one more good white shirt would do ya.

That's who Demeter was talking about. "He's messed with me one time too many. And I'm done with it! ... You want to know about the first time? Well, I was just an innocent filly back then. I had gotten to that age when all the young fellas in town were looking at me with a gleam in their eyes. And I tell you what, honey, I did enjoy it.

"And then, *he* began to notice me. Everybody but me knew it was just a matter of time. Sure enough, one evening he came up behind me as I was walking along that path up there past the big house. He started talking real sweet to me. He said it sure was a hot night, wasn't it? He allowed as how he had a freezer of homemade ambrosia ice cream up at his house and nobody to share it with him. He said he'd be mighty pleased if I'd come up and sit a spell on his porch and have a bowl of that ice cream. He said it would be a pleasant way to cool off, wouldn't it?

"Honey, he knew how to push my buttons, because there ain't nothing I like more than homemade ambrosia ice cream—unless it's pomegranate pie. So that's how he got me to go home with him. And let me tell you, honey, there wasn't any ice cream up there. You know what I'm saying?

"So after that was when my daughter Persephone Korene was born. I've always called her Korey for short. It was such a beautiful time when she came into the world. The first flowers began to bloom, but my baby girl was prettier than any of them. She was a good girl, too. I never had any trouble with that girl. She was always singing and smiling. Having Korey to love helped me forget about Old Zeus. I just wish he had forgotten about me. I just wish he had stopped messing with my life."

We sat there on that tree stump for a while without making a sound. I thought I saw tears starting to well up in her eyes. I wouldn't have left her then for anything in the world.

In a bit, she started talking again. "Let me tell you about the next time. I had just started to go out and have a little fun again. I went to a barn dance over in the next county, and I was having the best time I'd had in years. I'd been dancing all evening with this really nice fella. You might call him a hayseed, I reckon, but I was fond of him and hoping we would see each other again. Maybe it was the moon or maybe it was the moonshine, but the next thing I knew, we were sitting under the stars kissing. You know how it is when you're young and you think you're in love? What a night. I'll never forget it. And I won't ever forget what happened afterwards either.

"Old Zeus always had a way of finding out about things that were none of his business. He found out about my new boyfriend. Yasius was his name. Well, Old Zeus didn't care for Yasius or his people. They were Titans, but Old Zeus called them 'white trash.' He told me not to hang around them any-more, just like he owned me or something. By the next morning, Yasius had disappeared. He was just nowhere to be found. Some folks swore to me that they had seen a flash of lightning come out of that big house. They said it hit Yasius and he just vanished into thin air. I believe it. Old Zeus would do some-thing like that if he was mad.

"I never did get over losing Yasius.

"After that, I just poured all the love I had into Korey. She was the smartest little girl. She could figure things out that lots of kids her age wouldn't have a clue about. Take the time—I guess she was about ten years old—we were walking along that path up there by the big house. She stopped, tugged on my dress, and said, 'Mama, how come you never talk to me about Papa Zeus?' So I sat her down right here on this tree stump. I told her the whole story. I told her about being a woman, about the joys and sorrows. I explained how sometimes something good can come from something bad, like she had come to me. And then I warned her not to ever let anybody mess with her life. I could tell she understood. She knew it was important to look out for herself.

"That's why, honey, when she turned up missing a few days ago, I knew something was suspicious. Old Zeus tried to tell me she had probably run off with some sweet-talking white trash like I had nearly done. But I knew better. She wouldn't do something like that. I know my Korey. So I kept searching until I found out the truth. And when I did, it made my blood boil. She hadn't been sweet-talked into running off. She was kidnapped!

"Some of her friends saw it happen. They were out in those fields with her gathering wildflowers. Suddenly this fancy black carriage came barreling over the horizon, almost as if it had come right up out of the ground. Then a strange man dressed all in black jumped out, grabbed Korey, and rode off with her screaming her lungs out.

"Now let me ask you something, honey. How is it that a fancy carriage like that could show up in these parts without Old Zeus knowing about it? And why wouldn't he use his thunderbolts and lightning to zap somebody who was stealing his own child right out from under his nose? I'll tell you why. Because Old Zeus was in on it! That stranger dressed in black? Why, he was none other than Zeus's very own brother—Hades!

"You ever heard about him? He's a sorry excuse of a creature. Odd as a two-dollar bill. He never did like it up here on the earth. Couldn't tolerate the fresh air and sunshine. So he took his share of the family inheritance and built himself an underground kingdom—his own private little hell. And that's where I believe he has taken my daughter. I told Old Zeus that, and he just laughed about it. Acted like it was a joke. But he knows it's true. And *he* knows that *I* know that *he* was in on the whole thing.

"So now, he can sit up there in his big ol' house and look out on his fields going to dust and his crops withering, and there ain't nothing he can do about it. He's gonna learn that I've got some power of my own. As long as my Korey is gone, this land ain't gonna bear nothing for nobody. You got that, honey?"

Yep, I allowed as how I did.

As Demeter looked away from me, I saw that the tears were gone and that other look, the one I first saw, was back. She began staring out over the fields again. I decided it was time for me to go. I eased up off that stump and walked aways up the road. When I was out of earshot, I turned and looked back. I saw acres and acres of dry fields. I felt a cold wind starting to blow. And there sat that attractive yellow-haired lady with a hard look on her face. I said to myself, "Now that is one angry woman."

It was several weeks later when I found out how things turned out. It wasn't exactly a happy ending for Demeter, but in this world, a woman has to take what she can get. Eventually Old Zeus gave in. He couldn't stand seeing his land dying. So he prevailed upon his bother Hades to release Korey and allow her to return to her mother—but only for half the year. Because of some kind of deal those brothers cooked up—something about Korey eating a few seeds while she was down in Hades' place—the poor girl has to go back down and spend the other half of the year with Hades.

I sure felt sorry for Demeter when I heard about that. I knew how much it meant to her to get her daughter back. And I knew how painful it would be to lose her again.

Do you have any idea how strong a mother's love for her child is?

Well, one day in spring, you just look outside at the crops and the wildflowers growing. You listen to the birds singing, feel the gentle breeze and the warmth of the sun ... and you'll understand something of the joy and love a mother feels for her child.

Then you look back out there on a bitter winter day. You see how stark and desolate the fields are, how dead the grass and trees look. You feel the cold wind blowing around you ... and you'll begin to know the emptiness in a mother's heart when her child is taken from her.

And then remember this: A mother's love is as endless as the cycle of the seasons.

# MEDEA

Medea? She was the nicest girl in town back when we were growing up in Colchis. Oh, nobody liked it much when she started messing with that voodoo magic. But that was her daddy's fault. He was an amateur magician, crazier than a peach orchard boar, and always trying to pull the wool over somebody's eyes. How he ever got to be mayor of our town is a complete mystery to me.

But Medea ... she grew up right gentle, and pretty too. I used to see her coming out of their big ol' house every evening about dusk, wearing a starched white dress, her long black hair flowing down her back. She was the closest thing to a goddess I ever did see. She'd go off into the woods to gather herbs and crystals and tree bark—whatever she used in those potions she concocted. She could've had her pick of any man in the county, but she didn't seem much interested in men. Until that lousy Jason came along.

Now you know I would rather walk on my lips than criticize somebody, but that Jason was rotten to the core. And if he wasn't bad enough, that uncouth bunch of jocks that tagged along with him were nothing but a bunch of worthless yahoos. I don't know where he found those guys. They were always looking for some free food and wine. Not one of 'em ever did a day's work that I saw. And whaddya know, they showed up in our town to get the only thing we had that was worth anything: the Golden Fleece!

See, once there was this golden ram. When it died, somebody skinned it, and thus the Golden Fleece. Our town won the fleece from the Greeks in some kind of a contest. At least, that's the story I heard. So that fleece became our little town's prized possession.

Anyway, that pack of hooligans floated up on a big boat called the Argo, surfed ashore, and told everybody they were the Argonauts. Any idiot knows that Argonaut just means somebody who sails on the Argo. But they seemed real proud of the name, like whoever thought it up was a genius. I tell you what, those boys had some good-lookin' bodies, but not one of 'em had an IQ bigger than his neck size. Then they started spreading it around town that they were going to take the Golden Fleece back to Greece where it rightfully belonged. What they didn't tell us was that the governor back home had promised Jason a major political appointment in exchange for the fleece.

Well, our mayor, Medea's pop, wasn't much on civic pride, but there was no way he was gonna let those Argonauts take something made of solid gold out of our town. He would've been more than a match for the whole boatload—if it hadn't been for Medea.

Now I know that you've heard a lot of dirt about Medea. I'll be the first to admit that some of it is true. But most of it is pure hogwash. What really happened was that Medea had a nervous breakdown. And it was that no-good Jason who drove her to it.

After that, she did do some terrible things. But I'll get to that part later.

Where was I? Oh yeah. So when the mayor got wind of those Argonauts bragging about their mission, he invited the whole gang up to his house for a party. He told 'em he'd be glad to give 'em the Golden Fleece, but first, he had a couple of chores he'd like for 'em to do. Farming—sort of. He had an acre that needed plowing, and he had just the oxen to do it. After that, he had a few seeds to be sown. What Jason didn't know was that those oxen breathed fire. We are talking industrial-strength flamethrowers! One snort and they could burn everything within a mile radius to a crisp. And those seeds the mayor wanted them to plant? They were serpent teeth. Once planted, they'd grow up an army that would attack whoever was doing the planting. That would've wiped out Jason and his whole bunch of jocks in a matter of minutes.

But when Jason walked into the mayor's house that night, Medea looked at him and one of Cupid's little arrows went right through her heart. You know how it is with a woman's love. It's like the morning dew. It's as likely to fall on a horse turd as on a rose. Love can make a woman do some crazy things. Of course, Jason noticed Medea too, but it wasn't love he had in mind.

When Jason heard the mayor's proposal, he said, "Sure, no problem. Me and my boys will just yoke up those oxen and get the plowing and the planting done by noon tomorrow. Then we can pick up the Golden Fleece and be on our way."

That night Medea struggled with her feelings. On the one hand, she had a fierce loyalty to her daddy. On the other hand, Jason was a real hunk. She had never seen hair that blond or that curly before. And she liked the way his skin was bronzed from the sun and how those muscles rippled across his sculptured back and arms. But for some reason, beyond his looks, she was sure he was the man she'd been waiting for.

She finally made up her mind what to do. Here's where her finesse with magic came in handy. She went down to the basement laboratory and mixed up a potion that would knock your socks off. She worked on it all night. Just before dawn, she went to Jason and his boys and told them that the damage Sherman's army had done to Atlanta was just a pimple compared to what the mayor's bovines were gonna do to them that morning. She said if Jason would cover his entire beautiful body with her potion, he would be totally bulletproof and fireproof for one day. And if he would throw these stones she gave him into the ranks of soldiers that sprang up from the serpent teeth seeds, they would turn on each other and kill themselves. But, she said, looking apologetically at the crew, she'd had time to make only enough potion for one person.

The Argonauts said, "Aw, shucks! OK, how about if we wait a mile or two away? We only came along for the food and wine and parties, anyway. We don't want any trouble. Personally, we don't care one way or the other about that golden wad of sheep hair."

Sure enough, that morning everything went down just the way Medea said it would. And Jason, who otherwise would have made an ash of himself, walked away from the whole thing a hero. But the boy didn't learn a thing! He thought it was over and he had won. He went to the mayor and asked when he could pick up the fleece and be on his way. The mayor, speaking through clenched teeth, said he'd be making a formal presentation of the Golden Fleece the next day, with a banquet and speeches and such. But, he said, if Jason was in a big ol' hurry, he could go ahead and pick it up anytime. It was out at the edge of town.

In actual fact, the mayor had developed a new foolproof plan to get rid of those Argonauts. If they spent the night, he would kill them in their sleep. If they tried to pick up the fleece early, they would have to deal with Old Sleepy.

Old Sleepy was a great big lizard who lived right next to where the Golden Fleece was kept. Back in his younger days, he was as friendly and helpful a lizard as you'd ever meet. If you wanted the fleece, he would've been happy to help you carry it off—*if* you could catch him when he was awake, which was hard to do. Sleeping was his main deal. But one day a couple of years back, the mayor got a bright idea. He mixed up a potion that kept Old Sleepy from sleeping ... at all ... ever. So the worse that lizard's insomnia got, the more irritable he became. Eventually he was so aggravated, if anybody even came near his house, which was right next to the Golden Fleece, he'd just as soon eat 'em as look at 'em. And I am talking a big lizard here.

Medea found out about her daddy's plan. And she had a recipe for a potion to use on Old Sleepy that would counteract her daddy's potion. But it would take her about seventy-two hours to prepare it. And a sleepover for the Argonauts was out of the question. Jason was in big trouble.

Well, whaddya know. One of the Argonauts had the solution. A skinny guy who looked a cut above the rest of Jason's scurvy crew stepped out of the crowd with his guitar. He said his name was Orpheus, and he claimed he had a version of "Lullaby and Good Night" that was dynamite. He said he'd be glad to try it out on Old Sleepy. Well, it worked like a charm! As soon as Orpheus started strumming, that big lizard closed his eyes and hit the hay like a ton of bricks. Meanwhile, Jason and Medea grabbed the fleece and high-tailed it out of Colchis with the Argonauts putting the mettle to the paddles.

All the way back to Greece, those dumb clucks kept running into trouble. Every time they'd find themselves hip-deep in alligators, they'd go crying to Medea for help. She bailed 'em out time after time. But when they finally reached their hometown, Iolcos, those nitwits never even stopped to thank her. They scattered to trade their tall tales for some free food and wine.

As for Jason, he kept on whining to Medea. The truth is, he couldn't find his way to the men's room without Medea's help. For instance, he was real surprised when the governor of Iolcos, who was glad to take the Golden Fleece off his hands, reneged on his promise to turn over the government to Jason. I wasn't surprised. Medea wasn't surprised. You're probably not surprised. But ol' pinheaded Jason was surprised!

He got madder and madder about it, but all he could do was think up nasty things he wanted to happen to the governor. Jason didn't have the brains to make any of them happen, of course. So he went whining to Medea, and she told him to relax and she'd take care of everything.

Medea knew that the governor used a ton of stuff like Rogaine and Grecian Formula 44 to hide his age. To say that he was vain would be a gross understatement. Medea arranged a meeting with the governor's daughters and told them that she had developed a wonderful fountain-of-youth potion. She said it trimmed years off a person's age and restored all the energy and vitality of the springtime of life. She demonstrated by putting Jason's senile daddy in a big pot of boiling water with some of her special magic herbs. To everyone's surprise and amazement, the old feller kicked the lid off and jumped out of that pot looking fifty years younger. The governor's daughters were real impressed. So they talked the governor into letting Medea put him in a pot of boiling water. Guess what? No magic herbs this time! Medea and Jason had to hot-foot it outta town before the governor's daughters took the lid off the pot.

Jason and Medea settled down in Corinth for a few quiet years. Medea was happy. She had all she'd ever wanted—Jason and a couple of fine sons.

But was Jason happy? Noooo! That dipstick wanted more! He started cheatin' on Medea. She knew it, of course, and it was getting on her nerves, but she stifled herself.

Then one day Jason came home late and said to her, "Guess what, sweetie pie! I am gonna marry President Creon's daughter. Just business, of course, nothing personal. I can still come by and see you on Thursday nights, because she thinks that's my poker night. And I think I can slip away most Sunday afternoons to take the boys to the park. Whooee, I'll have a lot of money and power now! Good news, huh?"

Medea gave him a look that would stop a speeding bullet. She said *no*, this was not the best plan for the future she could imagine. She said something about when you go to a party, you are supposed to dance with the one that brung you.

Jason didn't get it.

He ran back to the president and told him that Medea didn't seem thrilled with the current plan, and the president got worried that he might not be able to marry off his daughter as quickly as he had hoped. So President Creon sent a message to Medea that read something like this: "You and yore young'uns git the hell outta Dodge within twenty-four hours, or yore dead meat."

Well, Medea, who was smart about everything—except Jason—decided that all she needed to do was talk to Jason and everything could be straightened out. She invited him over for coffee, and she reminded him of a few things. She asked him to recall how she had taken care of the fire-breathing oxen and the serpent-teeth soldiers, all the while betraying her own daddy so that Jason could steal the Golden Fleece. So you see, she could never, ever go back home to Colchis. And, of course, after she had helped Jason get revenge on the governor, she couldn't go back to Jason's hometown, because the governor's daughters would rip her to shreds. And now she was being exiled from Corinth. All of this happened because she loved Jason and would do anything in the world for him—except lose him. She said, "Can't we work something out, honey?"

That's when old Jason-the-Jerk sat her down and explained a few things to her. He said she got as good as she gave. He said that he had mentioned to *several* people that she had helped him a tiny bit with the Golden Fleece. Most every time folks praised his heroic deeds, he gave her a little of the credit. He didn't have to, he was just that kind of guy. Why, he had personally taken her off the farm and moved her to the big city so she could be cultured and have a sophisticated life. If it hadn't been for him, she wouldn't have amounted to a hill of beans. *She* was the one who had betrayed her daddy and killed the governor and PO'd the president. It wasn't his fault that she had gotten herself exiled. If she had just been a good sport about his wedding, she wouldn't be in this mess!

That's when Medea lost it. That was the beginning of her nervous breakdown.

She gave Jason a great big smile and said he was right, as usual. She said he should just run along and get ready for his wedding while she finished up a gift for him and then packed for her exile. Maybe they could do lunch soon, she said. Bye-bye, and have a nice day.

Medea went to a trunk and took out a beautiful gown encrusted with gold and jewels. She stroked it lovingly. Then she placed it in a gift box, sprinkled a magic potion over it, and laughed softly. She put the lid on the box and gift-wrapped it.

Then she called her sons and told them to deliver the gown to the president's daughter. She instructed them to wait and see ... uh, if the gown might need to be altered. The boys did exactly what their mama said.

The bride-to-be loved the gown, and it fit perfectly. But just as she was telling the boys to say "Thanks a lot" to their mama, she noticed she was having a bit of trouble breathing. Suddenly, her skin began to burn, and she started screaming. The president ran in to see what was happening. He tried to pull the dress off her, and then he caught fire and started screaming too. There were flames and smoke everywhere. By the time somebody came to help them, they were nothing but a pile of ashes on the floor.

The boys ran home and told their mama what they had seen. Medea listened carefully. "That's a shame," she said. "What a pity."

Then Medea held her sons close and said she needed to tell them something very important. "There are some things worse than dying," she said. "People without a powerful protector can be enslaved and ridiculed by their enemies. They live in shame—and death is better than that."

And then very quickly—oh, I wish I didn't have to tell you this part, but I've got to—she stabbed her sons, her own sweet boys, each in their heart.

Then in a daze, she gathered her belongings, saddled her horse, and escaped Corinth before anybody could put her away. She ran from place to place, but she got kicked out of every town where she tried to take up residence. She kept getting crazier and doing mean things just for the fun of it, or so it seemed. But that mean, crazy woman wasn't the real Medea. Not the one I grew up with. She was a different woman after she had that nervous breakdown, and I'll always blame Jason for that.

That night she killed her sons, she struck a hard bargain with herself. To do what she did, she had to forget for just one minute that they were her beautiful babies. They became, in her mind, nothing more than Jason's link to posterity. A man is nothing without descendants. That's what we were always taught when we were growing up. Medea traded herself one moment of amnesia for a lifetime of revenge. After that, she had no choice but to stay crazy so she could live with herself.

I hope you'll think more kindly of Medea now that you know what really happened.

# THESEUS

Theseus is a Greek word that means "forgetful."

OK, so it's not, but it ought to be.

When Theseus was born, his daddy picked him up, turned him around a few times, looked deep into his eyes, and said to the mama, "Hon, this boy's got a few cogs without a matching ratchet." Now, he could have said a lot of things that would have become self-fulfilling prophecies about Theseus. He could have said:

"This boy is about half a bubble off plumb."

"This boy's elevator don't go all the way to the top."

"He don't have both oars in the water."

"He ain't playing with a full deck."

"His lights are on, but he ain't home."

"He ain't huntin' with all his dogs."

"He's a few bricks shy of a load."

"He's a couple of cookies short of a dozen."

"He's a taco short of a combination plate."

"He ain't the sharpest quill on the porcupine."

"There ain't no pilot in his cockpit."

"He don't have syrup between all his pancakes."

"His dipstick don't reach his oil."

"He don't sit on a stool with both sides of his cheeks."

"The wheel is turning, but the hamster is dead."

"If you put his brains in a bee, it would fly backwards."

"If his IQ slips any lower, we'll have to water him twice a day."

"It takes him an hour and a half to watch '60 Minutes.'"

"His head ain't warm all the way around."

*Or* ... "He must have gotten into the gene pool when the life-guard wasn't looking."

He could have said any of those things. But what he said was, "This boy's got a few cogs without a matching ratchet." And the daddy was right.

Then the daddy took a sword and a pair of shoes, buried them in a hole in the back yard, covered them up with a big ol' rock, and said to his wife. "Hon, when this boy gets big enough to move that rock, and smart enough to know what's under it, send him around to see me." And the daddy was outta there!

The mama did the best she could raising Theseus. He grew into a great big strapping boy. But by the time he was a teenager, he was starting to get on his mama's nerves a right smart. That boy couldn't remember anything she told him. Besides that, when it came to following directions, he was slower than a herd of turtles stampeding through peanut butter. Every day the mama would say, "Son, do you remember that hole out there in the back yard?"

"Uh, sure, Mom."

"Well, go out there and see if you can move that rock off it."

"Sure, Mom."

But before he could get all the way out to that rock, he would trip over an anthill and lose track of where he was going. Or he'd get caught up in a game of "Gotcha" with his friends and forget all about what he was supposed to be doing.

You see, "Gotcha" was Theseus's favorite game, and he whiled away many an hour playing it. It's still a popular game today in a few remote locations. This is how it works: everybody, except the one who is It, goes out into the woods and hides up in the trees. The one who is It then walks under the trees looking for the ones who are hiding. Suddenly somebody up in a tree jumps down on the one who is It, knocking the one who is It to the ground, sometimes rendering the one who is It unconscious. The one doing the jumping then hollers, "Gotcha!"

Theseus loved being It. He was so good at being It, everybody let him be It all the time. He would go walking along under those trees and somebody would jump down on him. But Theseus always heard them before they landed on him. He could hear the leaves rustle. He could hear the air move. So before anybody could lay a hand on him, he would whirl around, knock 'em about a hundred yards, and holler, "Gotcha back!"

Theseus's mama would see him dragging back in the house a few hours after she'd sent him out, and she'd say, "Are you coming back in here without that rock?"

Theseus would wrinkle up his brow like he was working on a problem in quantum physics and say, "What rock?"

The mama would say to herself, "This boy's got a few cogs without a matching ratchet." She could have said a lot of things. She could have said, "This boy couldn't find his rear end if it was on fire." But what she said was, "This boy's got a few cogs without a matching ratchet."

One day, the mama got fed up. She grabbed Theseus by the ear and dragged him out to the back yard.

"*That* rock, son. Do you see that rock?"

"Uh, sure, Mom."

"Well, move it!"

"Sure, Mom."

Theseus didn't know how strong he was. He picked up that big ol' rock with one hand and tossed it aside.

"Now, what do you see down there in that hole?" asked his mama.

"Uh, a sword and a pair of shoes."

"Congratulations, Son. You pass with an A."

The mama slapped a map into one of his hands and a sack lunch into the other. "Good luck with your daddy," she said. And the mama was outta there!

Theseus's daddy had taken up residence in a place called Athens, so that's where Theseus headed. The Athenian Road was a very dangerous road. It was infested with a bunch of ragtag, third-rate burglars and bandits with names like Procrustes and Periphetes and Sinis. They hid in the bushes and trees alongside the road. When wayfarers went down that road, carrying suitcases, pushing baby buggies, those creeps would jump down on 'em, rob and terrorize 'em, and generally act like hoodlums. Well, when the terrible stories about the road made the front-page news, people were afraid to travel to Athens anymore. They stayed home rather than take their chances on that highway of horror. But what did Theseus know about current events? Diddly squat! But luckily, this situation was made to order for Theseus's unique talents. He went merrily down that road, and when those burglars and bandits jumped down on him, he heard the leaves rustle and the air move. He whirled around, knocked 'em about a hundred yards, and hollered, "Gotcha back!" Those perverts were never seen again, and the Athenian Road became a shining example of early urban renewal.

Well, when word got out in Athens about this big hero who was coming to town, folks turned out to cheer his arrival. Meanwhile, Theseus's daddy, Aegeus, who was now king of Athens and enjoying the company of a girlfriend named Medea, got very worried. He had no idea that the road hero was his very own son. Medea, who did not have a stellar reputation in family relations, convinced Aegeus that this hero might be elected the new king of Athens and that poor ol' Aegeus would be left crownless, powerless, and penniless. So she hatched a plot to poison the mysterious hero.

When Theseus got to town, Aegeus and Medea greeted him at the city gates and handed him a cup of wine. "A toast to your bravery," cooed Medea, looking Theseus up and down. When she got to his eyes and looked deep, she said to herself, "Hmm, this boy's got a few cogs without a matching ratchet." Now she could have said a lot of things. She could have said, "This boy couldn't drink beer out of a boot if the instructions were printed on the heel." But what she said was, "This boy's got a few cogs without a matching ratchet."

As Theseus tipped the beverage to his lips, Aegeus recognized the sharp sword and the dusty shoes he had buried so long ago. He realized that this hero was none other than his abandoned son. Aegeus knocked the cup of poison from the boy's lips and embraced him. "My son, at last I've found you!" Medea lost control of herself (not a new experience for her) and made a rapid exit from town (also not a new experience for her). Meanwhile, Theseus and Aegeus enjoyed a wonderful family reunion and did some serious male bonding.

It so happened that these were tough times in Athens. A few years back, Athens had gotten into a scuffle with the island of Crete. The Athenians had lost. So now every nine years, as payment to the King of Crete, Athens was required to send seven young men and seven young women to Crete, where they were fed to a monstrous Minotaur. When Theseus heard of this atrocity, he said, "Hey! I've got a swell idea! I'm a big-time hero. How about if I go along on the boat this time and just kill that ... uh ... that ... Whaddya call that thing? Oh, yeah, Minotaur! Yep, I'll just kill that Minotaur. No problem. Well, so long. See you later ... uh ... see you later ... Whaddya call yourself? Dad! Yep, see you later, Dad!"

The next day, Theseus joined the thirteen other adolescents bound for Crete. The ship was launched under black sails, befitting the occasion. But Theseus promised Aegeus that if the mission was successful, they would return under white sails. Aegeus could look out over the water and know before the ship ever reached shore whether or not his son was alive.

When the ship reached Crete, it docked in the massive, ultra-modern harbor, designed by an architect named Daedalus. The young Athenians went ashore, led by Theseus. The first person who greeted them was a beautiful island girl who fell in love with Theseus the moment she laid eyes on him. She looked him up, and she looked him down, and she liked what she saw. Then she looked deep into his eyes, and she said to herself, "Mmm, this boy's got a few cogs without a matching ratchet." Now she could have said a lot of things. She could have said, "This boy couldn't find his zipper if it had flashing lights on it." But what she said was, "This boy's got a few cogs without a matching ratchet." Theseus was her best hope, so the girl tried not to think about the consequences.

Now this girl was no run-of-the-mill citizen of Crete. She was Ariadne, daughter of King Minos and half-sister to the Minotaur. She walked along next to Theseus and explained to him about the labyrinth where her daddy kept the Minotaur. She told him she was certain that he was strong enough to destroy the Minotaur. But, she said, he could never find his way out of that labyrinth without a little help from her. She'd be happy to provide some assistance, explained Ariadne, if he would take her with him as his wife when he left Crete.

"Sure, Mom ... uh, sure, Dad ... uh, sure, Ari-something. Sure, take you with me ... whatever."

When they reached the entrance to the labyrinth, Ariadne handed Theseus a golden ball of string. She told him to let that string unwind behind him as he made his way through the maze of passages. Once he killed the Minotaur, all he had to do was follow the string back to her. She said she'd be waiting with her wedding dress and her running shoes.

Theseus led his not-so-merry band of thirteen through the door of the labyrinth, unwinding the golden string as he went. The passageway was dark and dank and narrow, twisting and turning back on itself like a snake. When they reached the innermost part of the maze, Theseus felt the movement of air above him. The bull-headed monster jumped from his hiding place on the wall overhead, snorting and spewing phlegm on the intruders. But Theseus, anticipating the attack, stepped aside and whirled around, and before the Minotaur could lay a hoof on anybody, Theseus knocked him about a hundred yards. "Gotcha back!" he yelled. The Minotaur lay dead, deader than a doornail.

Theseus sat down on the lifeless body of the monster and pouted. "Shucks. Now how in the name of Sam Hill are we supposed to get out of this lousy place?"

His friends looked deep into his eyes and said to themselves, "This boy's got a few cogs without a matching ratchet." They could have said a lot of things, but what they did was yell real loud, *"The string, stupid, the string!"*

Theseus looked down at the ball of string still in his hand.

"Sure. Right. I knew that. I was just checking. Come on. Follow me. I'm getting you people outta here!"

They picked up Ariadne at the door, ran for the harbor, and sailed away from the island of Crete at full speed. That night they stopped to rest on the island of Naxos. Ariadne unpacked her wedding frock, and she and Theseus were married by the local justice of the peace. It was the shortest honeymoon in history. Before the crack of dawn, Theseus loaded the crew and the bags back onto the ship and set sail for Athens. Not far out of the harbor, one of his shipmates looked back and yelled, "Ariadne! Theseus, you forgot Ariadne!" Sure enough, there she stood, knee deep in the ocean, still in her nightgown, frantically waving her arms.

"Who?" said Theseus. "Ari-who? Oh yeah, her. Nice girl. Well, home to Athens. Full-speed ahead!" Would you believe it? He forgot about her. Went off and left her and forgot all about her. And that wasn't even the worst thing that happened that day.

As the ship approached Athens, Aegeus was standing on a high, rocky cliff gazing out over the horizon. When he saw the vessel, he began to weep, and he threw himself to his death on the rocks below. You want to guess what color the sails were? That's right—black. Theseus forgot to change them!

That's how the rest of Theseus's life went. One faux pas after another. He messed up so many times, nobody bothered to keep track for posterity anymore. He got married three more times ... or maybe it was four. I can't remember. Neither could he!

Once, he went down to the underworld, thinking he could rescue a beautiful woman named Persephone. Hades caught him, of course, and punished him by making him sit in the Chair of Forgetfulness. What a hoot! Theseus felt right at home. He sat there looking mellow, forgetting who he was and what he was supposed to be doing. But, you see, that Chair of Forgetfulness was a fiendish device. It not only took away your memory, but it also sealed itself to your rear end like Super Glue. Theseus would still be there if it hadn't been for his pal Hercules who followed him down there, grabbed hold of him, and ripped him out of that chair, leaving part of Theseus still attached. That's why, by the way, to this very day Theseus's descendants are known as "half-ass people."

How that boy Theseus ever got to be a hero to the Greeks is a complete mystery to me. On the one hand, he screwed up just about everything he touched. On the other hand, he did clean up the Athenian Road, and he did rid the world of the Minotaur, and he did bring those thirteen young people home safe to Athens. So I guess you could say he did the best he could for a boy who had a few cogs without a matching ratchet.

# BACCHUS

Bacchus drank too much. Everybody knows he drank too much. What did they expect, for crying out loud? He was the god of wine, not the god of mineral water. But when folks know about the tough time he had getting born and growing up, they're willing to give him a little slack for leaning on the grape juice too hard.

What some people don't understand is that Bacchus was a half-god. That was his daddy's contribution. His daddy was Zeus—the *número uno* on Mount Olympus, the chairman of the board, the head honcho. Zeus controlled everything around him, except his wife, Hera. She was a mean-mouthed woman. Hard as woodpecker lips. Wore barbed-wire underpants. Put on her earrings with a staple gun. Hera didn't trust Zeus, and with good reason. Zeus had a girlfriend in every port, and Hera knew about them, of course, because knowing stuff was her business. She had spies everywhere, the sneakiest of them being the Titans, who loved to see Zeus get himself in trouble. Mostly, though, it was his girlfriends who got punished because Hera never could figure how to get the best of her two-timing mate.

One sweet young thing who had fallen in love with Zeus was a mortal named Semele (pronounced around here as Simma Lee). She didn't know that her beloved was none other than the god Zeus, because he always came courting in disguise. He had to. For starters, he kept trying to fool Hera, which he never did. But also, there was the safety of his non-Olympian paramours he was concerned about. You see, if a mortal looked at Zeus in all of his magnificence and splendor, she would have an electrifying experience. Literally.

Well, after a time, Semele discovered that she was expecting a child. She was thrilled. Hera heard the news from one of her Titan spies. She wasn't thrilled because she knew exactly who the daddy was. Hera dressed herself up like a kindly neighborhood granny and went down to visit Semele.

"Oh, honey, good news about your baby! Who is your boyfriend? No, I mean, who is he *really*? I can see you're not sure. Well, if he loves you, he'll tell you. Better yet, get him to take off that silly Zorro disguise he wears and show you his true identity. Trust me, honey, you'll get a charge out of it."

So the next time Zeus came around to visit, Semele said she had just one wish. She persuaded Zeus to take an oath on the River Styx that he would give her that one wish. Her wish was for him to reveal his true self to her. What a pickle Zeus was in. Styx River oaths were sacred and irrevocable. He peeled off his disguise and poor Semele burst into flames and was fried to a crisp.

Zeus snatched up Semele's unborn child from the mother's smoldering ashes. Then Zeus cut a gash in his own upper thigh, put the baby into the wound, and sewed himself back up. That's how baby Bacchus spent his prenatal period—safe and snug right next to his pop's Fruits of the Loom.

A few months later, Zeus gave birth, in a peculiar sort of way, to his child of fire. He tried to keep it a secret, but the Titans, using their most effective Gestapo tactics, got hold of the story, gave it to the tabloids, and then kidnapped Baby Bacchus. Those Titans were not the least bit culturally flexible. Delighted to follow Hera's terrible orders, they tore Bacchus to shreds and boiled him. Luckily, Bacchus's grandma, Rhea, a woman of true grit, found Bacchus in the crockpot. She spooned him out, pieced him back together, and sent him off to live with Semele's sister, his Aunt Ino.

Dear Aunt Ino did everything she could to protect little Bacchus from Hera. She dressed him in her daughter's clothes. She let his curly hair grow out long and tied ribbons in it. She pinched his chubby cheeks to make 'em pink and taught him how to say, "Oooeee, I love shopping!" But Hera eventually ferreted him out. She turned Aunt Ino into a real nut case. The poor woman started running around in circles, her head turned backwards, slobber dripping off her lips, her eyes spinning around like a cartoon character that's been hit upside the head with a board. She totally wigged out! It was a sad sight. Hera claimed Aunt Ino was an unfit surrogate mother, and that she herself would take custody of the child.

Zeus finally got over his postpartum depression and intervened. Using a little hocus pocus, he changed Bacchus into a goat—temporarily, just long enough to confuse Hera and slip Bacchus off into the woods. Zeus left the boy there to be raised by nymphs.

Thus it was that Bacchus spent his youth doted upon by physically gifted women who enjoyed a clothing-optional lifestyle. He was home-schooled—typical of a New Age living environment. The muses and the satyrs taught him poetry, music, and dance. His private tutor Silenus, an odd old character who was half horse and half human, taught him wisdom and virtue.

In his spare time, Bacchus took up agriculture and learned how to grow grapes. He marked his passage from adolescence to adulthood by inventing wine. It was a lovely thing, that wine. Having learned from his teachers the virtue of generosity, he shared his wine with others. He taught people how to party. And Bacchus himself was the life of every party. Mortals came to depend on him to make good times happen. A bunch of dull people with the emotional range of pet rocks could get together and spend the evening boring the shoes off one another. But if Bacchus showed up and joined them, a warm and wonderful party would transpire. He could turn anybody, even computer programmers and accountants, into party people!

Besides being the god of wine and partyology, Bacchus was also the god of women. For a guy, he had unusual sensitivity about females. He'd drop by and say to an ordinary housewife, "Hey! You deserve a break today." He made you want to throw down your apron, peel off your pantyhose, and go running barefooted through the woods with him. Lots of women did that very thing. They were driven by pure ecstasy. He'd say, "Stop and smell the roses, girls. Full many a flower is born to blush unseen and waste its sweetness on the desert air."[1] All the women loved it when he talked like that, because they knew he was sincere. He understood their needs. They went home from an afternoon with Bacchus feeling appreciated.

Bacchus married only once. She was the lovely Ariadne, daughter of King Minos and former wife of Theseus, the twit who abandoned her on the island of Naxos after one day of marriage. Don't get me started on him! Anyway, Bacchus rescued Ariadne from Naxos and was faithful to her until the day she died. In her memory, he placed a crown among the stars in the sky. It's called the Corona Borealis. Isn't that just the sweetest thing you ever heard?

And did you know, Bacchus went to hell and back for his mama? Yes, ma'am, rescued her from the land of the dead. He made a deal with Hades, went down there and got her out, and took her up to Mount Olympus to live under Zeus's protection—a mortal among gods. Gave Semele back the life she had lost. Such a son, a real mensch!

The goddess Hestia, the peacemaker in Zeus's family, admired Bacchus so much for being a stand-up guy, she persuaded Hera to end her war of vengeance on him. Then Hestia offered Bacchus her seat at the Olympian board table, right next to Zeus. People who say that Hestia wasn't politically savvy don't have a clue!

Well, that's the life of Bacchus ... in a grape seed, more or less. There are a lot of folks today who will tell you that he was an immoral drunk who was unkind to animals, made women wild, and ran naked through the neighborhood. But that's just not true.

Oh sure, Bacchus drank too much. Everybody knows he drank too much. But he survived a rotten childhood, he loved his mama and his wife, he treated all women like first-class citizens, and he knew how to help everybody have a good time. And I ought to know. I threw down my apron and ran through the woods with him on more than one occasion. I like to remember him as the god of wine, women, and whoopee. Cheers, Bacchus!

# JUDGMENT OF PARIS

Eris was a troublemaker. She had a mean streak a mile long. If there was a rumor to start or a back to stab, she was first in line. Most people knew what she was like, and they didn't want to have anything to do with her.

Well, there was this nice lady—nobody today even remembers her name—who was giving a wedding party, and she didn't want any trouble at that party. So she invited everybody except Eris, the goddess of discord. "So what if Eris gets mad?" that nice lady said to herself. "What baaaaad could happen?"

At first, things were going just fine at the party. All the party-goers were holding up their little fingers while they ate their onion dip. They were all dressed fancy and they talked polite. And then ... Eris showed up at that party! Eris was as clever as she was mean. She had this golden apple that was so enticing you couldn't look at it without wanting to touch it, to hold it, to own it. She inscribed on that apple: "For the fairest." She opened the door and rolled the golden apple into the center of the party. One woman picked it up, held it high so everybody else could see, and then she read the inscription aloud: "For the fairest."

The ladies at that party were on that apple like a pack of hound dogs on a coon. You've never seen such eye-scratching and hair-pulling as went on there. All those women clumped up around that apple, fighting for it. They formed a huge human ball. That ball began to roll across the floor. You could see an arm stick out here, a leg poke out there. Every one of those women was yelling and cussing at the top of her lungs. They knocked over the buffet table and smashed the bar. It looked like somebody was gonna have to use a fire hose to break 'em up. But before long, the stronger ones started pitching the weaker ones through the windows, through the doors, through the walls. Then it got down to just three women, each with a white-knuckle grip on that apple. Their heads were real close together, their brows furrowed, their teeth clenched. They were muttering things to each other, obviously trying to work this deal out in a ladylike fashion. Finally, they looked up to Zeus on Mount Olympus and demanded, "Settle this for us!"

Well, Zeus was no fool. If he made one woman happy, he made two enemies for life. It didn't compute. Besides, he knew plenty about those three women who were struggling for that golden apple.

First, there was Hera. Politically, she was the most powerful woman on Mount Olympus. Besides, she was his wife, and she could hold a grudge longer than anybody.

Second, there was Athena, the goddess of war. At a whim, she could change the course of battle anywhere in the world.

And third, there was Aphrodite ... which rhymes with nightie. She wore this magic golden girdle that made any man who looked at her fall madly in love with her. She was, of course, the goddess of love.

Zeus looked down at those three women looking up at him, and he declared, "I'm too busy to mess with this. I'll get you somebody else to settle it. After all, what baaaaad could happen?"

Right here is where a guy named Paris comes into this story. Paris thought he was a shepherd. He lived on the side of a mountain and he took care of sheep, so what was he supposed to think? The truth is, he was the son of the king of Troy. Back when Paris was born, an old oracle said that Paris was gonna be nothing but trouble and would eventually bring down the whole city of Troy. So Paris got thrown out of town, and ended up herding sheep on the side of a mountain.

You can imagine Paris's surprise that day when Hermes, Zeus's messenger boy, showed up with those three gorgeous goddesses. "Uh, let me get this straight," said Paris. "You want me to decide which one of these women is the fairest?" Now you gotta understand, Paris didn't get off the mountain much. And there wasn't a video store or a magazine stand or a singles bar within a hundred miles of there. "Judge a beauty contest, huh? Sure, I can do that! After all, what baaaaad could happen?"

"That remains to be seen, Mr. Paris," said Hermes. "Now, will you be judging the contestants in evening gowns, swimsuits, or disrobed."

"Dis ... uhhh, you mean ... as in naked?"

"Certainly, Mr. Paris. It's customary."

"Well, I'm not as dumb as I look. I believe I'll judge 'em disrobed."

"Your choice, Mr. Paris. Like you said, what baaaaad could happen?"

Before the beauty contest could get underway, a scuffle erupted. Aphrodite tried to leave on her magic girdle, but, of course, that would have caused Paris to fall in love with her. So Hera held her down, and Athena ripped it off her. Then Athena insisted that she had to wear her hat, a military-style helmet that everybody recognized as her trademark. "No way!" yelled Aphrodite, jerking it right off Athena's head. Now she'd have hat-hair and couldn't possibly win. Finally the beauty contest began. One at a time, the goddesses came before Paris.

Hera danced for Paris. Her skin was so fair she was known as the "Goddess of the Ivory Arms." Then she leaned over and whispered in his ear, "How would you like to be president of this whole world? I have connections. I can make it happen."

"Nah. I got all the sheep I can take care of now. If I was president of the whole world, I never would get all them sheep out to pasture and back. I don't want to be president, but you sure are a pretty girl!"

The next to come before Paris was Athena. To tell you the truth, she didn't like disrobing in front of anybody. But she desperately wanted that golden apple, so she tossed aside her toga and started talking. "Paris, my dear boy, you can just forget about old 'Fish-Belly Arms' and 'Girdle Gut.' What do they know about gifts for a real man like you? You choose me as the fairest, and I'll make you the greatest warrior of all time. With me on your side, you will never lose a battle."

"Nah. I don't like fightin' all that much. There's a big ol' goat herder that lives on the other side of the mountain, and he tries to beat me up every now and then. Most of the time, I just out-run him. But you sure are a pretty girl!"

The last goddess to parade before Paris was Aphrodite. She sized up the situation real quick. "Listen up, shepherd boy. How would you like to make whoopee with Helen of Troy?"

"Bingo!" hollered Paris. "You're the prettiest girl I've ever seen!" And he tossed her the golden apple.

Aphrodite grabbed that apple, tucked it safely under her arm, and went off to make arrangements for Helen to be kidnapped by Paris. Meanwhile, Hera and Athena decided to do lunch and plot the destruction of Troy.

Well, that's how the Trojan War got started. It lasted for almost ten years. The great city of Troy was demolished and many lives were lost. If only that nice lady who gave that wedding party and shunned the goddess of discord could have known ... what baaaaad *could* happen!

# ODYSSEUS AND ACHILLES: DRAFT DODGERS

You probably already know that some people are born great, and some people achieve greatness, and some people have greatness thrust upon them. What you may not know is that two of the greatest heroes of the Trojan War were thrustees.

The war started when Paris, a Trojan, kidnapped Helen, a Greek, and carried her back home with him to Troy. Greece decided to send out a thousand ships to get Helen back. Yep, that's right. One thousand. I know what you're thinking, and I don't understand it either. One boy loses control of his hormones and a whole country gets plumb bent out of shape and starts a war. Makes no sense, but that's what happened.

When the Greeks got ready to launch their thousand ships, they noticed they were missing two draft dodgers. One of them was Odysseus. Now, Odysseus was brave, clean, and reverent. He also had a pretty good imagination and a lot of common sense. He had a little farm, a lovely wife, and a fine young son. He just didn't want to go fight that crazy ol' Trojan War. Besides, he knew that Helen had been carried off by some other lovestruck fool a few years ago. That time, a couple of her brothers went and got her. Well, if just a couple of guys could do it back then, he figured, maybe nine hundred and ninety-nine ships could pull it off this time. He'd stay home.

Odysseus knew that the draft board would come after him, but he was ready for them. He shaved his head and spray-painted it with purple and orange stripes. He applied black soot to his lips and eyelids. Then he tie-dyed some baggy clothes and put rips in them. He wore his underpants on the outside instead of where they should have been. He put a chain in his nose and an earring in his navel. (Little did he know that this look would catch on with teenagers a few thousand years later.)

When he saw the draft board coming, he went out to his field, got behind his plow, and started sowing salt. He walked along behind that plow, muttering to himself, spit running down his chin, a wild look in his eyes. The draft board looked at him real close and wondered if he was the best choice for a general of the allied forces in the assault on Troy. But one wise old cracker on the board figured out what was happening. He scooped up Odysseus's young son and plunked him down in the furrow Odysseus was plowing. Odysseus got closer and closer with those sharp plow blades. The board member held the boy firm in Odysseus's path. With one second to spare, Odysseus swerved the plow and missed the boy. He grabbed the boy and hugged him. Then he looked at the draft board ... and the draft board looked at him ... and with one voice the draft board said:

> You're in the army now,
> You're not behind a plow,
> You'll never get rich digging a ditch,
> You're in the army now!

After Odysseus was sworn in, his first job was to go after the other draft dodger. His name was Achilles.

Achilles had a mama who was somewhat overprotective. First thing, when he was born, she dipped him in the water of the River Styx. That made him invincible ... except for that little spot on his heel where she was holding him when she dipped him. Well, you'd think that was enough. You'd think his mama would just let him grow up normal, except for being invincible, and let it go at that. Au contraire, as we say back home. To keep Achilles from going into the army, she sent him to an all-girls school. He dressed in girls' clothes and took classes in sewing and cooking—not a politically correct thing to do back then. "Overprotective" may not fully describe the workings of the mind of Achilles' mama.

It didn't take Odysseus long to find out where Achilles was. Odysseus disguised himself as a peddler and went to that school. He set up his table in the courtyard and started laying out his goods. He had brightly colored hair ribbons and a nice assortment of sewing needles and thread. He had lovely laces and linen and silk. He also had some finely crafted daggers and a few swords with excellent balance and sharp edges. All the little girls came running out of the dormitory, oohing and aahing and giggling. They gathered around the peddler's table, trying on the hair ribbons, admiring the fabrics. All except for one little girl. She was checking out the balance on one of the swords. That little girl looked up at Odysseus and saw that he was looking right back at her. Odysseus smiled and said:

> You're in the army now,
> You cannot be a frau,
> You'll never get rich learning to stitch,
> You're in the army now!

Well, that's how Odysseus and Achilles became thrustees in the Greek army. They went off to fight in the Trojan War, and only one of them survived. You remember that little spot on Achilles' heel? Maybe his mama wasn't quite overprotective enough. After ten long and bloody years, the Greeks finally won. Without those two draft dodgers who ended up heroes, the Greek army wouldn't have had a chance. Just think, the course of human history might have been changed if only Odysseus and Achilles had known how to get to Canada.

# PANDORA

Have you ever been making up your bed or fluffing up your pillow, and you came across one of those little tags that reads: UNDER PENALTY OF LAW—DO NOT REMOVE? And you thought to yourself, "Who says? This is *my* pillow. I can rip this sucker off right now. Are the Pillow Police gonna come in here and arrest me if I do?"

Well, that must have been how Pandora felt about that box. The box had been a wedding present from Papa Zeus. It was a beautiful box, covered with gold and inlaid with jewels. It had a heavy lid held shut by a lock. And underneath that lock there was a tag. It read: UNDER PENALTY OF LAW—DO NOT REMOVE. And Pandora probably said to herself, "Who says? This is *my* box. Papa Zeus gave it to me. Why wouldn't he want me to look inside it?"

You see, Pandora had a problem.

It had all started years and years ago as a feud between Papa Zeus and the Metheus brothers. You remember the Metheus brothers. There was Pro—Prometheus. He was the oldest and the smartest. And then there was Epi—Epimetheus. He wasn't

71

the sharpest knife in the drawer, but he was real proud of his big brother. He used to say, "This here's my bro Pro. He's the brains in the family."

The Metheus boys were Titans, but they lived right alongside the mortals from time to time. They were fond of the mortals and liked to give them presents. That made the mortals worship the ground they walked on. One day Pro decided to give the mortals a present like they had never had before—fire! With fire they could warm their feet and eat cooked meat. The problem was, the only fire that existed was in Papa Zeus's barbecue pit up on Mount Olympus. So one evening while Zeus was out on an affair— of state—Pro slipped in the back gate and stole a red hot coal from the fire pit. He took it down and gave it to the mortals. Well, that made Pro a hero with the mortals, but it chapped ol' Zeus's hide.

And what did Papa Zeus do about it? He punished Prometheus by hanging him on the side of a mountain. Pro hung there all day long in the boiling hot sun. And he hung there all night long in the cold. Then in the wee hours of the morning an eagle flew up to him, sat down on Pro's face, and started to peck at his belly. She pecked and pecked until she plucked his liver plumb out. She swallowed it and took off. Poor ol' Pro had to hang there again all day long in the boiling hot sun and all day night long in the cold. He was miserable, shivering, liverless. But he didn't die. He couldn't die because he was immortal. So that night he grew a brand new liver. And the next morning, the eagle was back. She plucked out that new liver, ate it, and took off again. Well, that same old routine went on day after day, month after month, year after year! That liver-loving eagle thought she had a standing invitation for breakfast.

Even after eons of time had gone by, Papa Zeus still wasn't satisfied that the Metheus brothers and their pals, the mortals, had gotten their fair share of punishment for stealing his fire. If there was one thing Zeus was good at, it was revenge. That was when Zeus hit upon the idea of making a *woman*. That's right, the first mortal woman! Up until then the whole world was inhabited by nothing but the good ol' boys. Not a woman amongst them. Not one. How their toilet paper rolls ever got changed is a mystery to me.

Zeus went to his son Phestus, the blacksmith, and asked him to design a creature that would drive the good ol' boys on the earth real crazy. What Phestus built was a woman. He made her strong and he made her beautiful. Zeus made her smart *and* he made her curious. Then Zeus named her Pandora, which means "gift to all."

You getting my drift here? It was a setup right from the start! Papa Zeus gave Pandora that beautiful box, the one covered with gold and inlaid with jewels, the one with the heavy lid and the lock and the little tag. You remember the one: UNDER PENALTY OF LAW—DO NOT REMOVE. Then he sent her off to find Epimetheus and marry up with him. The moment Epi laid eyes on Pandora, he was in love. So they got married. She promised to love, honor, and redecorate. And she got busy straightening out his sock drawer and his life.

For the first couple of weeks, Pandora was so busy being domestic she didn't think much about that box. But when she figured out that housework was boring, she began to notice that box more and more. She took to dusting it every morning. She polished the jewels every afternoon. One day Epi came home from work early, and when he saw her fondling that box, he shoved it into the closet. "Whooeee, Pandy honey, don't mess with that box! That box is trouble with a capital T and that rhymes with P and that stands for ... uh ... for ..."

"Pooey!" said Pandora. She wasn't scared of that box. She was curious about that box. And she went right on being curious.

As soon as Epi went back to work, she took that box out of the closet and put it on the coffee table. She read the tag under the lock again: UNDER PENALTY OF LAW—DO NOT REMOVE. And she said to herself, "How come I can't open this box? It's *my* box. What could possibly be in here that Papa Zeus wouldn't want me to see?" She commenced to stare at that box for hours each day. Her eyes would glaze over and her jaw would go slack. She'd even talk to that box. She began to look just like a TV soap opera addict. But that box held more troubles than a whole year's worth of "The Bold and the Beautiful," "The Young and the Restless," "All My Children," and "General Hospital" combined. Before long, Pandora was plumb eat up with curiosity. Why couldn't she just remove the lock, lift the lid, and have a tiny peek? She wouldn't take anything out of the box and lose it, for crying out loud!

Well, like I said before, Pandora was smart. So she finally figured it out. "Papa Zeus put that sign on the box so that nobody else would mess with it *but* me. After all, it was my present," she thought. "It's a lousy job," she chuckled, "but somebody's gotta do it." She ran out to the garage and got a crowbar. She popped off the lock, lifted up the lid, and ... well, that's when it all hit the fan!

All the stuff that makes life miserable came jumping out of that box: Sickness, old age, anger, envy, and lust. Racism, sexism, terrorism, and tourism. Communism, capitalism, TV evangelism. Alcoholism, drug addiction, pornography, and censorship. War and bombs and nuclear waste. Cholesterol, hemorrhoids, PMS and the IRS. Ring-around-the-collar and the heartbreak of psoriasis. Oh yes, all of that stuff and much, much more came flying out of that box.

But there was one little misfit down at the bottom of the box. Her name was Hope. She really didn't want to join the others, but she felt an obligation to take a flying leap. Instead, she took a chance and yelled out, "Pandora! Get a grip, girlfriend! Shut the lid or I'm outta here!"

Just in the nick of time, Pandora got a grip on herself and slammed down the lid and Hope was kept safe in the box.

Under the circumstances, considering she was framed and all, I think Pandora did the best she could for us. You can blame her for your troubles if you want to. People have been giving her a bad rap for thousands of years. But when you're down-and-out and nothing else seems to help, just remember: there's always Hope. She's still there, waiting for you when you need her ... deep inside.

# MEDUSA

Did you ever hear the sad story of Medusa? She was the ugliest woman who ever lived. Why, she was so ugly ... she was so-o-o-o ugly ... "How ugly was she?" you ask. She was so ugly, if you looked her right in the face, you'd be turned to stone.

Yes, indeed, hers was a real sad story. Because, you see, she hadn't always been ugly. She started out with the looks of a goddess, so naturally she attracted lots of gods. Unfortunately, she got herself involved in one too many "dangerous liaisons," if you know what I mean. The last one was a fatal attraction. It was with Poseidon.

You've heard of Poseidon, the god of the sea, the one who ran around with a pitchfork in his hand, seaweed in his hair, and his participles a-dangling. Poseidon and Medusa rendezvoused one night in the nearest empty building they could find and had themselves a wild Olympic party. It turned out that the empty building was a temple of the goddess Athena, and when Athena heard about it, she was fit to be tied.

You see, Athena was the leader of the Mount Olympus

Moral Minority. She was always trying to improve the stan-
dards up there, trying to keep the neighborhood from going
downhill. She was also C.E.O. of the Evelyn Woods School of
Speed Revenge. Well, somebody had to be punished for defiling
her temple.

Poseidon had connections—he was Zeus's brother. Athena
couldn't touch him. But poor Medusa had no connections at all,
so she had to bear the full brunt of Athena's wrath. Athena
knew just how to put some serious hurtin' on a woman. She
took away her beauty—all of it. She made Medusa the ugliest
woman who ever lived.

Did you ask me how ugly she was? I really don't have words
bad enough to describe it, but this will give you some idea:

They say she had bulging red eyes that glowed in the dark,
enormous teeth that looked like fangs, and a huge tongue that
hung out of her mouth, over her chin, past her knees, all the
way down to her feet. It dragged along between her legs when
she walked. And her breath? Well, considering all the garbage
her tongue picked up, it smelled like a dog had died in her
mouth.

Let's not forget about her hair! Her hair wasn't just stringy.
Athena gave her snakes for hair! Dozens of self-willed little
strands, each one of them curling and coiling and hissing and
going its own way. You think you have bad-hair days? She
couldn't do a thing with that mess on her head. She tried it all—
mousse, gel, hot rollers, curling irons, perms. Nothing worked!

As for the rest of Medusa's body, Athena gave her hard,
scaly skin like a lizard, wings like a bat, and claws like a vulture.
Truly, she was the ugliest woman in the world.

But the worst part was what the ugliness did to her social
life. Oh, at first there was a brief period when she was something of a celebrity. Stories about her were splashed across the

front page of the *National Enquirer*. You'd hear people in line at the grocery store say, "Whooee, look at that—a story about 'The Ugliest Woman in the World.' Yessirree-bob, I want to see her in the flesh if it's the last thing I do." And if they did... it was.

Because nobody could look directly at Medusa and live to tell about it. One glance and you'd turn to stone. So, of course, nobody wanted to have her around anymore. Here she was, the original party girl, and now she couldn't draw flies at a picnic.

Her neighbors got up a petition to throw her out of town. There was nothing for her to do but pack up and go off to live in some desolate place where nobody would have to look at her. The gods allowed her two unattractive gorgon sisters to go along with her for company. (Did you ever notice how beautiful heroines, even formerly beautiful heroines, always have two nasty and unattractive sisters?) The three of them found a desert island and planned to spend the rest of their miserable days there.

Now right about here in a story like this you usually hear about a handsome young man—a prince, a hero—who chances upon the hapless maiden and changes her life. Yep, this story has a handsome young man, a prince and a hero, in fact. He chanced upon Medusa and changed her life. The truth is, she lost her head over him.

The name of this hero was Perseus. He began life not as a mere mortal, but as the son of Zeus. That meant he was only semi-mortal, and he was fated to do great things.

Perseus was born under unusual circumstances. His mother, Danae, was a princess who had a falling-out with her daddy, the king. It seems as how the king had a habit of visiting a place called Delphi to seek the advice of a fortuneteller called an oracle. Why he wasn't satisfied with relying on his horoscope like any normal head of state would do is a mystery to me. Anyway, this oracle told him that the son of his daughter, his own grandson, would kill him someday.

That put the king in a dither. He hurried home and he locked his daughter Danae up in a tower and forbade anyone, especially any men, to visit her. That way, she could never have a child. Right? Wrong! Because the king didn't count on the power of Zeus. You see, Zeus never could resist a damsel in distress—or a damsel of any kind, for that matter. Zeus paid Danae a visit in that prison tower. And soon after that, Danae gave birth to a son. She named him Perseus, which means "the Avenger."

Now her daddy the king had to fall back on Plan B. He figured out that this wasn't a normal birth, so he needed to be careful how he handled the situation. He couldn't just kill the baby and be done with the whole thing. Instead, he locked Danae and her baby in a wooden trunk and threw the trunk in the ocean. If they suffocated or drowned, it wasn't exactly his fault, was it?

But the gods look after the ones they care about. And the gods cared about this young son of Zeus. The trunk washed safely ashore in a distant land. An old fisherman found the mother and child and took them in. That old fisherman became like a real daddy to Perseus. And so it was that Perseus, the son of a god and the grandson of a king, grew up in a humble fisherman's shack. But his mother told him he was going to be a hero someday, and his first opportunity came just about the time most boys get their driver's license.

The king of this new land where they lived was named Polydectes. He decided he wanted to marry Perseus's mama. Polydectes was an evil dirt bag, and Danae didn't want to marry him, but she didn't seem to have any choice in the matter. The king went ahead and planned a bachelor party for himself. He invited all the men in the kingdom to come and bring him a present. Perseus went to that party, but he didn't take a present. He stepped right up to King Polydectes and promised to give him any present he wanted if the king wouldn't force Danae to marry him. King Polydectes was delighted. Here was his chance to get rid of Danae's snotty-nosed kid. "You're on, boy. Bring me the head ... of Medusa."

I told you Perseus was a hero, right? And you know the gods have a way of watching over their heroes. In this case, it was Athena whose ears perked up as soon as she heard the name Medusa. She was still ticked off at Medusa for defiling her temple, and she couldn't pass up another opportunity to get even with her. Athena decided to give Perseus all the help she could.

Athena sent Hermes down to outfit Perseus for his quest. Hermes explained to Perseus that this was a special mission and that it would require special equipment. He took Perseus to the Mount Olympus Laboratories and outfitted him in the latest high-tech adventure gear. He gave him wing-tipped sandals so he could fly, a helmet that would make him invisible, and a special sword that could cut through steel. For a shield, he chose one with a finish so bright it reflected images like a mirror. He explained that this would protect Perseus from the power of Medusa, because if you looked at her reflection and not directly at her, you wouldn't be turned to stone. Finally, Hermes gave Perseus a matching handbag—a Hermes handbag. But it was very special. It was insulated with magic to hold the bloody head of Medusa.

Perseus buckled on his wing-tipped Nike Air sandals and flew to the desert island where he suspected Medusa lived. He knew it was the right place when he saw a bunch of stone sightseers on the beach. He made his way through an overgrowth of trees and came to an old, rundown castle. Medusa must be inside because ... well, because he saw tongue tracks going up the steps.

It wasn't easy walking in backward while using his shield like a mirror, but he managed. He went down halls and around corners and, finally, he found her. Oh, gag a maggot. She was even worse than he had imagined!

Lucky for him, Medusa was asleep. There she sat in her Lazy-Girl recliner, drool running out the corners of her mouth, phlegm dripping off her tongue, snot oozing out her nose, and matter seeping out of her eyes. We're talking major ugly here! So he crept up on her, adjusted his rear-view shield, raised his sword, and *ka-chunk*—he chopped off her head. Mercy, what a mess! He had to feel back behind him and find that writhing head of snakes and put it in his magic handbag. Then he put on his helmet of invisibility so Medusa's sisters couldn't see him and pull him back down to the ground, and he was outta there.

When Perseus got back home, he discovered that that slime-ball, King Polydectes, had already reneged on their deal. Polydectes had convinced Danae that Perseus was dead and that she had to live up to their bargain by marrying him. Perseus arrived back in town just as the prenuptial celebration was beginning.

You can imagine Polydectes' surprise when he saw Perseus standing in the doorway of his officers' quarters. The king ordered all his soldiers to take aim at the boy and fire on command. But Perseus still had one more trick in his bag. Perseus said exactly what a lot of teenage sons today might say, "Go ahead, buttface, make my day!" (Of course, he said it in Greek, which sounds a lot less cheeky.) Then he whipped out the head of Medusa and held it high in the air. Immediately, Polydectes and all his soldiers were turned to stone.

The common folks rejoiced when they heard the news. Right

away, they elected Perseus their new king. Perseus said thanks anyway, but he'd rather be a full-time professional hero. So he turned the kingship over to the old fisherman who had been like a daddy to him.

Danae told Perseus he deserved a little vacation after all he'd been through. So the two of them took a cruise, one of those five-day, four-night deals, and ended up in the same country where Perseus had been born. Perseus didn't recognize it, of course, having left there when he was a baby. A big track meet was being held at one of the seaside resorts, and since the organizers recognized Perseus as a big-time famous hero, they invited him to enter the event of his choice. Perseus had inherited his father's skill at throwing things—you know how Zeus loved to throw thunderbolts—so Perseus entered the discus throw.

Nobody knows exactly what went wrong that day. Either Perseus's right arm was a little stronger than he thought, or the wind got hold of that discus, but that discus sailed into the grandstands and hit an old man right upside the head. It killed him instantly. Perseus reached the old guy at the same time his mama did. They rolled him over and looked at his face. Danae uttered just one word: "Daddy!"

And so the long-ago prophecy of the oracle of Delphi had come true. Perseus had killed his own grandfather.

And what about Medusa? Whatever happened to her? Well, that poor girl never did manage to pull herself back together. The best you can say is that her whole body was recycled. Medusa's head was used as a decoration for Athena's shield. Her skin was stripped off and sewn into chastity belts for an entire army of Amazons. Her blood was drained and bottled and advertised as an antidote for snake bite, or wrinkles, or right-wing extremism—whichever one scares you the most.

Some people even say that a few drops of her blood hit the ground and there sprang forth a magnificent winged horse called Peggy Sue. Personally, I think whoever dreamed that one up has a few screws loose.

One thing I do believe. Remember that old saying? Sure seems to ring true in this story: "Beauty is only skin deep, but *ugly* goes clear to the bone."

# CUPID AND PSYCHE

Cupid was a mama's boy. It wasn't his fault. She wouldn't let go of him. She practically hogtied him with her apron strings. You know how mamas are about their babies. So what if Cupid was already thirty-something! He would always be her own little cherub.

Cupid had a hard time shaking that image. Let's face it, Cupid has been the official poster child for Valentine's Day for several thousand years. Cute little naked baby, chubby cheeks, curly locks. Teeny-tiny wings, itsy-bitsy bow with miniature arrows. Goes around shooting people with his arrows, and they fall in love and live happily ever after. Sound about right?

Well, forget about it!

Cupid grew up a long time ago. Grew up tall, blond, and handsome. Still had those wings and still shot people with those love arrows. In fact, he was the god of love, but his mama's aprons strings were tying him down.

Cupid's mama was Aphrodite, and she had problems of her own. Years ago she had won a golden apple in a beauty contest, and she figured that settled the beauty question once and for all.

So if she heard of another woman who was supposed to be really beautiful, she'd pitch a fit. Then she'd send her son Cupid out to ruin that woman's life with his bow and arrows.

Let me tell you about the power of those arrows. If you got shot with one, you'd turn into a seething mass of desire, a hunka-hunka burnin' love. Then you'd start to put the moves on the very next creature you laid eyes on. Let's say you were out having a business lunch with your boss, and you got hit by one of Cupid's arrows. Because of the scene you'd make right there on the spot, you could lose your job—or get a great big pay raise. Either way, they sure wouldn't let you back in the Burger King anymore. You see what I mean about those arrows?

Well, there was a mortal girl named Psyche who was absolutely gorgeous. She had two older sisters. Remember the two sisters in "Cinderella"? How about the two sisters in "Beauty and the Beast"? OK, Psyche's sisters—same song, second verse. Anyway, Psyche was so beautiful people began to call her the "new and improved Aphrodite." That really got on Aphrodite's nerves a right smart. When her jealousy hit the overflow mark, she called to her son: "Cupid!"

"Yes, Mama?"

"Cupid, I need you to teach that little trollop named Psyche a lesson."

"Sure thing, Mama."

"I want you to shoot her with one of your arrows. And I want the next thing she sees to be the ugliest creature in the universe. She'll fall in love with it and live a life of shame, degradation, and misery."

"All right, Mama. How about a giant two-headed spider?"

"Not bad enough."

"How about a Cyclops?"

"Not nearly bad enough."

"A Minotaur, Mama?"

"Son, lots of women are married to guys that are half-bull, half-man! What I want is a Texas redneck. I want one with tobacco juice running out the corners of his mouth, a beer can in his hand, and his belly hanging over his belt. I want a muddy pickup truck with a gun rack in the back window and a big ol' hound dog in the front seat. Am I making myself clear, Son?"

"Yes, ma'am. I've never seen you this mad before, but you got it!"

Cupid found Psyche taking a nap beside a stream. He hid behind a bush, got his bow and arrow lined up, and waited for the first pickup truck to come along. Then Psyche rolled over and Cupid got a good look at her face. "Wow!" he said, jumping back. "This is one beautiful girl." As he jumped back, he stabbed himself in the leg with his very own arrow.

That was Cupid's first experience with the idea that what goes around comes around. He fell crazy in love with Psyche, but he couldn't do a thing about it because his mama might be watching. So Cupid hot-winged it outta there and hid for a while, trying to figure out how he could marry Psyche and still keep his mama happy—'cause if Mama ain't happy, ain't nobody happy. Meanwhile he laid some magic on Psyche so she would stay unmarried while he worked out a plan. He wasn't taking any chances on losing her.

Time passed and both of Psyche's older sisters got married to kings. Psyche was still as lovely as ever, but no suitors came to call. Psyche's parents got so worried, they went to an oracle—you know, a fortuneteller—and asked for advice. The oracle told them the sad and mysterious news: Psyche was destined to marry a non-human winged creature with a poisonous bite. The fortune included instructions to buy her a black wedding dress and leave her on a mountaintop where her husband could find her.

When the parents broke the news to Psyche, she began to weep quietly. Her two older sisters carried on like they really cared. "Oh, Psyche! What a shame. You have to marry a monster. Maybe it's a dragon. Maybe it's a great big snake. Married to a snake. Imagine that! What a shame, especially with you being so beautiful and all. We're real sorry. Well, goodbye and good luck. Maybe we'll see you later. Maybe not!"

Psyche put on her black bridal gown and was delivered to the designated mountaintop to wait for her husband. Suddenly a great wind swept her off the mountain and carried her to the place where her husband lived. It turned out to be the most luxurious place Psyche had ever seen. The facilities included exquisitely maintained gardens, crystal-clear fountains, and a magnificent palace inlaid with gold and silver and ivory. Within the palace was a twenty-four-hour gourmet kitchen. Invisible servants met Psyche's every need. And each night, in utter darkness, her husband came to Psyche's room, held her close, and told her how much he adored her. As kind as he was, he never allowed Psyche to see him. She promised she wouldn't try. Each morning, Psyche woke up smiling. Life just doesn't get any better than this, she thought.

Months went by, and one day Psyche received a note from her sisters. They wanted to drop by for a visit, someday when her husband wasn't home. They weren't fond of snakes, they said. That night in the darkness when she told her husband, he said to her, "Not a good idea. Those sisters of yours are just trouble waiting for a place to happen."

"Perhaps they've changed. Besides, they're family. You know what they say, 'You can pick your friends ...' Oh, never mind. Anyway, I miss them ... sort of. It's just a short visit. What bad could happen?"

"OK, but I hope you know what you're doing," said the monster-husband. "A word to the wise: If they try to talk you into taking a peek at me, don't do it. Otherwise, it's all over for us. I'm a very private person. I'm in a ... a witness protection program. You can love me without looking at me, can't you? Trust me on this."

The next day the wind shuttle was arranged and the two sisters showed up for their visit. They looked around at the facilities and said, "What's going on here? This place is ten times nicer than ours, and we're married to kings! Are you gonna try to make us believe you get all this from a snake? Never heard of a snake this rich. You sure he's a snake and not just some big west Texas billionaire trying to hide from the government? What's that you say? You've never even laid eyes on him because he only shows up here when it's dark? Oooo, baby sister, you *do* have a problem. Everything that goes around in the dark ain't Santa Claus. No telling what kind of a creep he is. You better get a look at this monster and terminate him before he does it to you first."

By the time the sisters left, Psyche was terribly upset and confused. She said to herself, "Maybe I need to shed a little light on this situation and snitch a peek at him. I know I promised I wouldn't, but what's he trying to hide?"

That night, Psyche took an oil lamp and a knife to bed with her. After her husband arrived and fell asleep, she got out of bed, lit the lamp, held the knife ready, and leaned over the sleeping form. "Wow!" she said, jumping back. "This is one good-looking monster! Wait a minute, this is ... it's ... no, it can't be. Cupid, the god of love? And he's mine?"

Now it so happened that while she was jumping back, Psyche sloshed the oil in that lamp. A drop of it ran down the side of the lamp and fell on Cupid's shoulder and burned him, ever so slightly. His eyes opened, and when he saw Psyche looking at him, he said, *"Sweetest things turn sourest by their deeds. Lilies that fester smell far worse than weeds."*[2] Which meant: "You didn't trust me, so I can't trust you, and now I gotta go."

Cupid flew out the window, and so did Psyche's happiness. She was miserable. Her curiosity and suspicions had ruined her idyllic life. The next morning, she set out searching for Cupid. She searched for days but found no trace of him. Finally, in desperation, she went to his mama for help.

Meanwhile, guess who was giving aid and comfort to her baby boy? Mama! And she began to suspect that his melancholy mood was more than homesickness. Eventually it dawned on Aphrodite that Cupid was pining for Psyche. She suggested that he take a vacation at one of her resorts and try to forget whatever garbage was cluttering his head.

The next morning when Aphrodite looked out her window and saw Psyche coming, she got mad enough to eat nails. By now she had learned all the details of Cupid's scheme to keep his marriage to this mortal a secret. Aphrodite said to herself, "I'll work this girl half to death and I won't feed her much. She'll get skinny and ugly and Cupid will forget all about her. Oh yes! The golden apple and my son are still mine!"

But what Aphrodite said to Psyche was this: "Sure, hon, I'll be glad to help you find Cupid. Tell you what, you do a few little tasks for me, and I'll put the word out to all my contacts. My sweet boy will be so happy that you came to see me."

Aphrodite took Psyche into a room where a huge box sat in the middle of the floor. "Look at this, hon. Somebody mixed up my grain shipment from Demeter. If you can get it all sorted into appropriate piles for me by morning, I'll see what I can do about finding Cupid." Aphrodite walked out and locked the door.

Psyche looked in that box, and it was full of cereal. There were corn flakes and bran flakes and wheat flakes. There were Sugar Pops and Cheerios and Count Choculas. There were Rice Chex and Grape-Nuts and bite-size, frosted Shredded Wheats. And they were in total disarray. Psyche took out a handful and began making piles. It seemed to take forever. She could never finish the whole box by morning. Just then, an army of ants crawled under the door. One tiny ant with sergeant stripes on its front legs stepped forward and saluted. "At your service, ma'am. Please step aside. All right, soldiers, let's move it!" Those ants formed themselves into twenty columns, scaled the side of that box, and began sorting the cereals. In short order, the job was done. Hmm, now who do you suppose was behind this helpful little trick?

Aphrodite walked back into the room the next morning and got so mad she wanted to slap Psyche into next week. But she didn't. Instead she gave Psyche two more impossible tasks to do, involving a herd of terrorist sheep who happened to have golden fleece and a goblet of mineral water located atop an ice-covered mountain. With the help of various species of talking plants and animals, sent by a certain secret pal, Psyche was able to pull off both jobs in record time.

Now Aphrodite was really harelipped! But she just smiled through her clenched teeth and said, "Psyche, go to Hades! ... and get me a box of beauty."

"I beg your pardon?" Psyche was certain she had misunderstood.

"Beauty. A box of it. Hades' wife, Persephone Korene, gets it for me wholesale. I'm feeling a little frayed around the edges, need to restore myself, so hurry and get back here with it. And whatever you do, *don't* open up that box and borrow any of my beauty. Maybe I'd better say that again, dear. *Don't* open up that box."

Psyche set off, looking for the road to Hades' underground kingdom. She passed a talking tower. What luck! The tower told her to take two quarters and three dog biscuits with her. "Never mind why, just do it !" said the tower as it pointed her in the right direction. She came to a river called the Styx. A ferryboat driver named Charon offered her a ride. Halfway across, he stopped the boat and held out his hand. Psyche placed a dog biscuit in his palm. Charon snarled, "Cut the funny stuff, lady."

"Oops! Sorry," said Psyche, switching the biscuit for a quarter. Charon then took her to the other side of the river, where she was greeted by Cerberus, a three-headed dog.

"Let me guess. Biscuits!" She tossed the doggie treats to the three heads and dashed through the gates to Hades' kingdom. She got the box from Persephone Korene and hurried out past the dog while the mouths were still chewing. She crossed the river, using her last quarter, and started up the road to Aphrodite's house. Along the way, Psyche said to herself, "I'm feeling a little frayed around the edges myself. I look like something the cat dragged in and the dog wouldn't eat. Cupid will never recognize me like this. I could use a little beauty right now. I wonder why I'm not supposed to open up this box?"

(Yo, Psyche! Does the name Pandora ring a bell?)

Psyche went right ahead and opened up the box ... and there wasn't any beauty in it at all! That box was full of eternal sleep. The sleep jumped out, grabbed Psyche, and she dropped like a rock.

Now who do you suppose had been watching and providing assistance to Psyche all this time? Yes, indeed, it was ol' Mama's Boy himself. He had gotten himself some therapy and decided it was time to cut the apron strings. He went straight to the board of directors on Mount Olympus and got their stamp of approval for his marriage to Psyche. They even granted her immortality—a favor rarely given to a human. They also instructed Aphrodite to find herself a new project! With the bargain made, Cupid flew down to Psyche, wiped the sleep from her eyes and put it back in the box. Then, ever so gently, he nicked her with his arrow. (Guess he wasn't taking any chances.) He looked into her eyes and said:

> *Love is not love*
> *Which alters when it alteration finds.*

And Psyche smiled at him and said:

> *O no; it is an ever-fixed mark,*
> *That looks on tempests, and is never shaken.*[3]

And that's the way it's been from that day to this for Cupid and Psyche.

# DAEDALUS AND ICARUS

Daedalus was a dreamer. Went around with his head in the clouds and his feet never quite touching the ground. He couldn't actually fly, of course, not back then, but his mind did soar. He was brilliant, in an oddball sort of way. Maybe too brilliant for his own good. You know how it is with geniuses. Creativity and common sense don't occupy an equal number of brain cells in their heads. Daedalus was like that—overloaded on creativity and short-sheeted on common sense.

He started inventing things before he could talk. He invented stuff nobody back then even had a use for. Take the time he carried his mama's hair dryer outside, sat on the side of the road, and pointed it at all the chariots passing by. Told everybody it was a prototype for radar. They didn't have the slightest idea what he was talking about, but they did slow down to gawk. Then there was the time he drew up the plans for a flying machine called a "Helios-copter." Folks laughed and said nobody in their right mind would give a wooden drachma for it. Finally he came up with an idea that sold. He designed a pair of wing-tipped sandals. Called them Nike Airs. Hermes, one of

Zeus's boys, bought the patent and took every pair he had.

Sometimes Daedalus's inventions were dangerous. He tried building a ski lift to Mount Olympus, but Zeus zapped it out of commission with a thunderbolt. Then he came up with a design for a new kind of temple in Athens. It had a glass roof. That way, Daedalus said, folks bringing their sacrifices could look right up at the gods and see what kind of mood they were in. The city government gave him the go-ahead, and he got it almost built and was putting on those glass shingles when a powerful rainstorm blew up. If he'd had any common sense, he would have figured out that it was a warning from Zeus about voyeurism. But Daedalus kept on working. He had his young nephew up there with him, doing all the tricky corners and edges. Well, the wind picked up the nephew and flung him to the ground. Broke his neck. Everybody said it was a bad omen from the gods, so the city council fired Daedalus and kicked him out of Athens.

The place where he finally found a welcome mat was the island of Crete. The royals there weren't famous for their family values. OK, let's face it, they were totally dysfunctional—a bunch of freelance fruitloops with bizarre passions. The king figured he might be able to capitalize on Daedalus's creative genius, so he gave him a job as the palace fix-it man.

The queen, Pasiphae, was an attractive woman, but King Minos was so busy with his intern-training program at the castle he hardly found time for the queen. She was pushing middle age and pushing it hard. Pasiphae was insecure and lonely and looking for a new interest in life. That's when she got into leather. You see, the king had a prize-winning bull that he kept in the pasture out back of the palace. It was, indeed, a fine-looking bull. It was pure white with shiny black hooves. It had a heavy gold ring in its nose and a brass bell around its neck. In many ways, it was a well-endowed bull.

Queen Pasiphae decided to attract the bull's attention. She convinced Daedalus to design her a cow suit. When she slipped into that suit, she was transformed into the loveliest cow in the kingdom, figuratively speaking. Daedalus even fixed it so that she smelled like a cow. She strolled into the pasture, blinking her big cow eyelashes and wagging her tail, and when the white bull got a look and a whiff, he went flat-out crazy. He started pawing the ground and snorting profusely. His eyes got verrrry big. He whistled at that gorgeous new cow and commenced sweet-talking her: "Hey, hey, hey! What's a good-lookin' heifer like you doing all alone in a place like this? Wanna ringy-ding my bell?"

That was the beginning of their courtship. The bull never caught on that she wasn't really his kind of girl, and the queen was just happy to have somebody's undivided attention for a while. It was a real shock to King Minos some time later, however, when Queen Pasiphae gave birth to a baby—a very peculiar baby. It was a fine strong boy ... mostly ... except for the head. It had a bull's head. What an embarrassment to the royal family. I know it's hard, but try to imagine: an ugly little prince with oversize ears, lots of big teeth, and an extremely snotty disposition. And someday, he would grow up to be king! Minos was ready to throw the baby off the balcony, but the queen calmed him by saying that, except for the head, that little fella looked very noble. Very strong and virile like Minos himself. In fact, she said, she planned on naming the child "Minotaur," sort of an affectionate bovine form of Minos.

For a while, to the outside observer, everything seemed hunky-dory in the palace. Nobody in the kingdom suspected that the newborn wasn't kosher. Queen Pasiphae covered up the little prince's head with oversize baby bonnets. But when the prince began snorting and demanding raw meat for breakfast and acting bullheaded, things got dicey. King Minos called on Daedalus for some design work. He asked Daedalus to draw up the blueprints for some sort of living quarters for this monstrous child—his own spacious apartment with a private entrance and no exit.

Daedalus came up with an ingenious plan. He designed a labyrinth, a maze that twisted and turned back on itself like a snake. It was a prison without guards. Daedalus was the only one who knew the secret of its passages. The Minotaur was ushered inside, and there he lived in seclusion. He had visitors only once every nine years, when fourteen youths were sent into the labyrinth. The Minotaur ate them. It was a special event, sort of a holiday, the only one he could look forward to.

One year, on that long-awaited feast day, a group of fourteen sacrificial adolescents showed up from Athens. They were sent as retribution for a battle the Athenians had lost to the Cretans. Their leader was a reckless young man named Theseus. You may recall that Theseus was the sort of kid a parent might be more than willing to sacrifice to a monster. Theseus wasn't exactly the sharpest quill on the porcupine, but he did have chutzpah. He marched into the labyrinth, killed the Minotaur, then ran off with the Minotaur's half sister, Ariadne, the lovely daughter of King Minos.

In truth, King Minos was relieved to be rid of his embarrassing stepson. But he despised the notion that he had been tricked, as well as robbed of his beautiful daughter. Somebody would have to pay for this unfortunate mess.

Well, who else? Daedalus! He was the one who had designed the cow suit and the so-called escape-proof labyrinth. Let him suffer for the king's misfortunes!

Meanwhile, Daedalus had developed a successful business in Crete called Designs by Daedalus. He had invented everything from hot tubs to zippered suits of armor. He had married a Cretan woman and had a Cretan son. In short, he was living in tall cotton. And then King Minos yanked him up, along with his teenage son, Icarus, and threw the two of them in jail. At first, Daedalus thought it was temporary insanity on the part of the king. Surely he would come to his senses and release Daedalus and the boy. But King Minos was looking for revenge, and he had found his scapegoat.

As the days and weeks went by, Daedalus began to suspect that the king had no intentions of releasing him. Daedalus offered Minos designs for new inventions, anything the king's heart desired, in exchange for freedom. The king ignored him. "Then let my boy to return to his mama," begged Daedalus. "He is of no use to you." But Minos kept the two of them locked securely in the prison tower.

One night, as Daedalus sat in his cell reading out-of-date newspapers declaring, PRINCESS FLIES THE COOP, his gaze fell upon the wax dripping from his candle. A scheme began to form in his mind. The next day he coaxed birds to the windowsill, using scraps of food as bait. He plucked a feather from each bird's wing. He collected and hoarded feathers, day after day, along with wax from the candles. Ever so carefully he fashioned huge wings for himself and Icarus. When they were completed, he strapped the wings onto their shoulders, removed the bars from the window with a makeshift lamb-bone hacksaw, and gave his son aerodynamic advice. Now keep in mind that this is Daedalus talking here—the former Mr. Head-in-the-Clouds himself giving a lecture on common sense to a boy who had not yet even owned a personal set of wheels and now had the latest model in wings.

"Follow right behind me, Son, but no tailgating. Stay in your own lane and no passing, yellow line or not. Keep your speed under the legal limit. No swooping and diving. Stay away from the sun and the saltwater. Avoid attracting the attention of the authorities. Yield at triangular signs. Don't color outside the lines. Don't run with a sharp object in your hand. And don't chew with your mouth open." (Parenthood requires otherwise intelligent grown-ups to say dumb stuff like this.) "When I say 'Fly,' you say, 'How high?' Here we go now, Son. Flap! Flap hard! Up, up, and away!"

Believe it or not, those wings worked. Daedalus and Icarus soared like seagulls, away from the island of Crete and across the Aegean Sea. In no time at all, they would reach freedom on the mainland. And then, Icarus forgot—or ignored—his father's advice. He took a sharp dive toward the water. Ah, how good it felt! He made a swoop toward the sun. He thrilled at the warmth and the danger. Suddenly he was out of control, laughing, doing spins and loops, tilts and whirls. Daedalus called out a warning: "Son, straighten up and fly right!"

But the words were wasted. The wax on the boy's wings began to melt. The feathers, heavy with water, drooped and loosened and fell. Icarus panicked, then plunged headlong into the cold ocean below. Eventually the feathers floated to the surface, but Icarus was never seen again.

Daedalus flew on and found refuge in a place called Sicily. He hung up his wings and never put them on again. Oh sure, he was a mortal and he had flown. It was an accomplishment he never took lightly. But he was also a father, and he had failed, and that forevermore weighed heavy on his heart.

Since that time, the story of Daedalus and Icarus has been told over and over again. And every parent who hears this tale knows the truth of it: it's a risky business giving a child wings.

# BAUCIS AND PHILEMON

Bacon. Mmm-mmm, bacon. Philemon loved bacon. Every morning he'd wake up with his old bones aching, and he'd say to himself, "I just don't think I can do it today." And then he would remember: Bacon! Mmm-mmm, bacon. If he could just manage to get himself out of that bed and check the nest of Agatha the goose for a fresh egg to round out his dozen, and if he could muster the strength to weed the garden and find a cabbage big enough to pick, then he would be close, very close, to having enough to trade at the market for a brand new slab of bacon. He had only a tiny piece of bacon left, and he vowed not to eat it until he had a brand new slab firmly in his grasp. Being completely without bacon produced in Philemon a sense of despair. He got out of bed gingerly and did what needed doing.

That night when he lay himself down next to his wife, Baucis, his old bones were aching bad as ever. They exchanged another day's happenings, and he reaffirmed his vow not to eat that last little morsel of bacon until he could bring home a fine new slab from the market. As the old couple drifted off to sleep, they were disturbed by the honking of their goose Agatha.

Somebody was at the door. Who could it be at this hour of the night? They were frightened, but they hurried to the door and opened it. Standing there were two handsome but roughly dressed strangers. They asked for food and shelter for the night.

"We have very little to offer," the old couple apologized, "but, yes, please come in!" Of course, these were guests. Guests, at any hour, were welcome in their home.

Baucis hurried into the kitchen and began to clean the last of their berries and radishes. Philemon took the head of cabbage he had picked that morning and put it in a pot of water to boil. It would have fetched a pretty penny at the market, but never mind. These were guests. Guests must always be treated with honor.

Baucis looked to the top shelf of the cupboard. That's where she kept the honey. Baucis felt about honey the way Philemon felt about bacon. But she had only a couple of tablespoonfuls left in the bottom of the jar. There were the bees and the bears who wanted that honey as much as she did, and she and Philemon were getting too old to run fast, so they hadn't gathered any in a long while. She looked from the jar to her husband and back to the jar. She nodded. Philemon placed the jar of honey on the table. And then Philemon dropped his last bit of bacon into the cabbage soup.

When they sat down at the table, Philemon reached for the serving spoon. He planned to divide the piece of bacon ever so carefully between the two guests. But the older of the two men quickly stuck his fork into the soup and lifted out the piece of bacon. It seemed bigger than Philemon remembered. The bearded guest stuffed the meat into his mouth, chewed, and swallowed. Philemon was mortified! Now what could he offer the other guest?

Before Philemon could think clearly again, the younger fellow poked his fork into the soup, fished around, and lifted out another piece of bacon! And it was bigger than the first one had been. He tossed the bacon into his mouth, chewed, swallowed, and grabbed the jar of honey. He tipped the jar and poured every drop, all two tablespoonfuls, onto his plate. Baucis turned scarlet and had trouble breathing. When she was able to focus her eyes once more, she looked at the jar and saw that it was now full to the brim with honey!

The old couple looked at each other, fell to their knees, and bowed their heads. "Forgive us, sirs. We did not know. We perceive now that you are gods. Forgive us for this humble meal. We gave what we had."

"Did you?" asked the bearded god. "What about your goose? She looks like a tasty morsel. Call her."

"The goose? Agatha, our watch-goose?" asked Baucis.

"Oh, surely not Agatha, the goose who provides us with eggs to trade for our bacon?" begged Philemon.

"The goose!" demanded the younger god.

"Very well ... the goose." And the old couple called for Agatha to come.

The older god, the bearded one, began to chuckle. "Just testing. We really don't want to cook your goose. Come with us. Please."

Quickly the two gods, none other than Zeus and Hermes, took Baucis and Philemon to the top of a hill overlooking the city. As they watched, a great flood descended upon the valley and destroyed every home, except for the hut of the old couple. Baucis and Philemon wept for their neighbors.

The gods explained, "We came to this city seeking only food and shelter, and everyone, except you, turned us away. You gave us the best you had. Now your home shall be a temple."

And as the old couple watched, their simple hut was transformed. The mud bricks turned to marble and the thatched roof changed to gold.

"Ask any favor, and it shall be yours."

Baucis and Philemon thought for a while. They had been married for many years and they had always been poor. Now they could have wealth beyond their dreams, honey that flowed, bacon without end! But at last they said, "We have shared our love and all that we have had for these many years. We know that we cannot live happily without each other. For now, let us gather the eggs and weed the cabbages—as best we can. Let us run with the honey from the bees and bears—as best we can. Let us enjoy our bacon—as often as we can! And then, when our time comes to die, allow us to die in the same moment."

And it was so. Baucis and Philemon lived happily together for many more years—as best they could. And when their time came to die, they joined hands.

There is to this very day, in that valley where they once lived, an old oak tree and a smaller linden tree. Their branches are intertwined ... and they grow from the same trunk.

> *That time of year thou mayst in me behold*
> *When yellow leaves, or none, or few, do hang*
> *Upon those boughs which shake against the cold,*
> *Bare ruin'd choirs, where late the sweet birds sang.*[4]

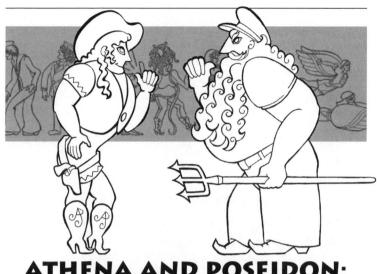

# ATHENA AND POSEIDON: THE LAND RUN

A few thousand years ago, the gods and goddesses of Mount Olympus had a land run a lot like the Oklahoma Run of 1889. The whole thing happened because some of the deities had started to argue about which parts of the earth were their patron territories. Zeus got tired of the bickering, so one day he told the gods and goddesses to line up. At the sound of his thunderbolt, they could run for whatever land they wanted.

It looked as though the race was a grand success. Apollo claimed his birthplace, the island of Delos. Demeter took Eleusis, a quiet land where she had found comfort when her daughter was kidnapped. Hades took Carlsbad Caverns and Wonder Cave, places where the sun don't shine. But about an hour into the race, a big fight broke out. Poseidon and Athena had chosen the same parcel of land. They each said they had staked their claim first. Zeus knew they were as stubborn as a pair of cross-eyed mules. Neither one would give in to the other. So Zeus had to get tough. "Chill out, both of you! We'll find a way to settle this in a civilized manner."

"Right!" shouted Poseidon. "A duel at sunrise."

"Great idea!" This came from Ares, the god of war. "I'll supply the weapons."

"Too dull," complained Athena. "Let's have a debate, a political-type debate."

"Nah, too nasty," whined Poseidon. "Let's just mud wrestle for this land."

Zeus had to think fast. He was losing control. "No, no. Debates, mudslinging—too common. It's been done. Not proper competition for deities. What we need is a dignified contest." Now he had their attention.

"OK, Chief," agreed Poseidon. "I'm all ears. Whaddya suggest?"

"Just name the terms," Athena dared. "I'll take him on."

Zeus calmly explained his plan. "Each of you is to provide this future city with a gift. Something special. All the rest of us will vote to determine which of you has given the best gift. The one who wins gets it all—lock, stock, and barrel. And the future city gets to keep both gifts. Beginning now, you have one hour to shop and come up with a gift. Meanwhile, I'll gather the family here for the vote."

By the end of the hour, all the Olympians were gathered and waiting. And there stood Athena and Poseidon, ready to bestow their gifts on the new city. Zeus flipped a coin to see who would go first. Poseidon won the toss.

Poseidon swaggered forward, glanced over at Athena, gave her a confident grin. Actually, it was more of a smirk. Then he raised his trident into the air and brought it down hard, thrusting it deep into the earth. Immediately there sprang from the ground a great torrent of sea water.

"Oooh, aaah," said the gods and goddesses. And they all applauded loudly.

"Nice trick, Poseidon," remarked Zeus. "But what good is it?"

Poseidon rolled his eyes and began to explain what it meant. "This is sea water, Chief. Get it? What is the most dangerous, most unpredictable realm in the universe? Why the sea, of course! The city that controls the sea controls the world. And that is my gift—control of the sea. Might makes right, and right makes rich, right? Sea power, that's the name of the game. And under my system, everybody benefits. It's called trickle-down economics."

"Oooh, aaah," said all the gods and goddesses. They really were impressed. This was a splendid gift. Even Zeus seemed awed by its magnificence. It didn't seem likely that Athena could come up with anything to match this. Zeus was tempted to call the whole thing off and declare Poseidon the winner. It would be such a shame to embarrass Athena. After all, she was his own daughter. But when he looked at her, he changed his mind. She was standing there, looking cool, calm, and collected—confident as ever.

Zeus muttered to himself, "She always has been a headstrong girl. She'll never admit defeat. I'll just give her enough rope and let her hang herself."

Zeus stepped forward, determined to lay on the compliments thick before she embarrassed herself. "And now, ladies and gentlemen, contestant number two. She hails right from the head of her daddy. She loves the spear and the shield. But she still has time for her favorite hobby—weaving. And let us not forget that she was valedictorian of her class at Mount Olympus High School. A big round of applause for a very talented little lady—Athena!"

Everybody clapped, and Athena stepped forward. She smiled at the crowd. Then she took from her robe, where she had been hiding it, her gift. Proudly, she held it aloft so everyone could see.

"Hiss! Boo!" said all the gods and goddesses.

Poseidon traded high-fives with Ares. He was sure he had won now.

Zeus looked flustered and embarrassed. He edged his way over to Athena, who was still standing there holding up her gift and looking triumphant. "Psst, Athena. You'd better come up with an explanation mighty quick, or you're gonna be the laughingstock of Mount Olympus."

"Why? What's wrong, Pop?" she asked.

"What's wrong? Well, we were supposed to have a real contest here. How do you expect to compete with a gift as grand as sea power when all you're giving is a ... a ... a potted plant!?" It was true. What Athena held in her hand was a small potted plant.

"Wussy gift, Athena babe!" shouted Ares. "Now all the ladies in Poseidonia, the new city of Poseidon, can have nice little potted plants to pretty up their houses. La-dee-dah!" But when Athena whirled around to face him and reached for her spear, he decided to back off.

"Oh ye of little faith," said Athena, "this is no mere potted plant." And then, glaring at Poseidon, she warned, "Watch and weep, pal!" Quickly she dug a hole and put the roots of the plant into the ground. Then summoning all the power that only a goddess can muster, she caused it to grow to full maturity in just a matter of seconds.

"Behold! The olive tree," she said.

A quiet "oooh, ahhh" came from Demeter. But nobody else had figured out what was happening.

"Let me tell you about the olive," offered Athena. "From the olive will come oil for cooking and for lighting homes. The olive tree will bring great wealth to this city. With that wealth, all the mortals here will live comfortable lives and will have time for learning, for music, theater, philosophy. So you see, from this simple potted plant, the olive tree, this city—*my* city—will receive the greatest gift of all: wisdom.

This time there was a loud chorus. *"Oooh. Aaah."* Then came the applause. It was thunderous.

Just to make sure, Zeus put it to a vote. Within seconds all the gods had gathered in a huddle around Poseidon. They were chewing and spitting and scratching. They started to chant, "Sea power, sea power, sea power." It wasn't so much that they liked Poseidon's gift better. They just hated to see one of the guys get beat.

Meanwhile, all the goddesses gathered around Athena and her olive tree. They admired the cleverness of her gift, how, from a living thing, from a green plant could come another kind of power: the power of wisdom. It was clear that Athena had all the votes of the goddesses.

So who won? You may recall that there were twelve Olympians: six gods and six goddesses. However, when the votes were cast, Zeus, as chairman of the board, abstained. Athena won six to five, by a show of female solidarity.

And what became of the new city? Well, you know its name. It was called Athens, the city of Athena. With the gift of Poseidon, it became the greatest of sea powers among all the Greek cities. But with the gift of Athena, it became a prosperous city and a center of learning. From Athens came the greatest thinkers and the finest philosophers the world has ever known.

And that's the story of the Olympian land run long, long ago. The grand finale was the founding of the magnificent capital of Athens—a city that learned to balance wealth with wisdom and power with peace.

Oooh! Aaah!

# POLYPHEMUS THE CYCLOPS

Polyphemus was a Cyclops with a serious eating disorder. He had an incurable appetite for human flesh. Oh, there had been a time when he was practically a vegetarian. Every now and then, on social occasions, he'd been known to have a wild boar burger or a few calf fries. But the fear of E. coli always sent him scurrying back to his vegetable garden. One day, that all changed. And now nothing could quite satisfy his taste like a well-seasoned and delicately roasted human being.

It all started on a stormy day when a ship was split apart on the rocks near his island. Polyphemus dived into the water, rescued the drowning sailors, swam back to shore, and deposited the bodies on the beach. The swim made the Cyclops hungry, and the day was still too stormy for harvesting his garden. He looked at his catch-of-the-day.

"Hmm, they're all soggy and hardly breathing. Not good for much ... except ... I'll just put them out of their misery." Polyphemus picked up a sailor and twisted his head like a bottle cap. Pop! Blood spewed into the air.

"Oops. Guess he was too shook up."

To stanch the geyser spouting from the decapitated body, Polyphemus placed his lips over the sailor's shoulders and sucked long and deep. "Yummm! Spicy! Italian!"

He quickly followed suit with the other sailors, placing the bodies in a neat pile on the beach and throwing the heads back into the water. "Brains are an acquired taste, I believe," he said to no one, for no one was left to hear him. Then he hurried back to his cave with his arms full of sailors. He built a fire, slipped the sailors onto a spit, and roasted them to a golden brown. Polyphemus ate greedily and, except for a passing moment of indigestion, experienced a gastronomic pleasure like none he had ever known before.

The next day, Polyphemus was back on the beach, waiting for another shipwreck. But the weather that day was mild, and ships sailed past the rocks on calm waters. For a week of days, Polyphemus sat on the beach, staring hungrily out at the smooth waters. His vegetables were of little interest to him now. He had a bad case of the post-human-consumption blues. And then his blues turned to anger. His temper became so savage the other Cyclopes on the island began to avoid him. He squatted on the beach each morning, cursing the clear sky. At last he muttered to himself, "When the going gets tough, the tough get going."

The next time he saw a sail in the distance, he swam to the ship, pushed it into a boulder until the vessel split, then swam back to shore with his pockets full of sailors. What a feast he had that night! This happened again and again, and Polyphemus enjoyed weeks of protein-rich menus—until word of his passion spread throughout the ports, and ships began to avoid those waters altogether. And so, for almost a year, Polyphemus was deprived of human flesh.

Meanwhile, in a not-so-faraway place called Troy, a war had ended. A surviving Greek general named Odysseus set sail with his men for their homeland. The gods of Mount Olympus, bored without the daily entertainment of battles, sent down a terrible storm and blew Odysseus's ship off course. The ship came to rest on an island that looked not only safe but fertile. The Greeks anchored their ship. Odysseus chose twelve of his men and announced, "Come on, boys, we're going ashore to find some groceries."

They soon discovered a cave with a gigantic stone blocking the entrance. The stone was ajar just enough that the Greeks could see a fire blazing inside. They heard the bleating of sheep. The men were cold and hungry. They squeezed past the rock and entered the cave.

Once inside, they found a huge fire pit, baskets of vegetables, a heap of decaying bones, and a pen full of shaggy sheep. Judging by the size of the cooking pot on the fire, Odysseus knew that whoever lived in this cave was either very large in number or very large in size. Then he heard a scraping sound, and Odysseus raced back to the door of the cave. The boulder had been rolled into place, and the opening was sealed shut. There was no way out.

The end of the cave where Odysseus stood was very dark. Far above him he saw a blinking red light.

Then he heard a voice. "Hello and welcome, my fine little human specimens. You're invited to stay for dinner, all of you." And then Odysseus saw fingers! Huge and hairy tentacles with filthy fingernails! He felt them clamp around his waist. He felt himself rising toward the blinking red light, which was, it turned out, a massive, bloodshot eye. Under it was a bulbous nose, dripping with the warm snot of anticipation. And beneath that was a grinning mouth, full of yellow teeth. Odysseus shuddered at the stench of Polyphemus's breath, but he didn't panic. The greater the danger, the better Odysseus's mind worked.

"Howdy, big fella. We'd be proud to share your table."

"Lovely! I am overjoyed. You have no idea how I have

missed human company this past year," said the grinning Cyclops. "Our menu this evening will feature Greek cuisine. It's what I call an interactive meal. Each of you will participate—in one course or another. Don't worry. No one will be left out."

Odysseus began to suspect double-entendre. "Reckon I'm a little slow on the uptake, big fella, but where in these parts do you find the necessary vittles for your Epicurean dining style?"

Polyphemus snorted with delight. "Oh, very near at hand, Captain." He reached down and snatched up a pair of Odysseus's men. He bashed their heads against the wall of the cave. He sucked out their brains—a taste he had, indeed, acquired. Then the Cyclops ate both men—clothes, skin, entrails, and all. He paused only long enough to crack open their bones and suck out the sweet marrow.

Polyphemus licked his fingers, belched, and spit out two pairs of shoes. "Forgive my manners, Captain."

"Oh, I hardly noticed," said Odysseus, trying to keep his knees from knocking. "Fingers were invented before forks. But personally, I'd recommend us well-done. No telling what sort of cooties we picked up back in Troy. Don't rush the main course. We'll be happy to wait. Can't be too careful when it comes to your health."

"Yes, yes, Captain, my sentiments exactly. I'll be outside picking some spices and herbs to season our dinner. Would you say that oregano is appropriate for Greek delicacies? Oh, what a feast this will be! While I'm gone, talk to your men. Tell them to cooperate. Tell them not to hide or run about the cave when their turns come up. If they are considerate, I'll be considerate in return. I'll unscrew their little heads or bash their skulls first, instead of cooking them alive. It's far less painful that way, Captain."

"You bet your boots, my good buddy. Take your time. I'll explain it to them," said Odysseus.

Polyphemus left the cave, securing the boulder behind him. Odysseus sat down by the fire, thinking up a plan. "Boys, we're on the horns of a dilemma here. Any ideas?"

One of the Greeks drew his sword.

"Naw, our swords are nothing but toothpicks for this monster." As Odysseus touched his own sword, he felt the wineskin at his side. It was filled with a wine so potent that even when mixed with twenty parts water, it put men quickly and deeply under the spell of Bacchus. Drunker than a skunk, in other words.

Then Odysseus saw a staff made of olive wood, left by Polyphemus in the sheep pen. It was long enough and strong enough to be the mast of a Greek ship. Now he had a plan! He ordered his men to draw their swords and shave the end of that staff to a sharp point. "When you're done, hide it next to yourselves at the back of that sheep pen."

"But sir," complained some of the men, "it stinks something awful back there. That's the location of the ... the dung pile."

"Yep," said Odysseus. "And we're gonna use it to our advantage. Keep saying to yourselves: dung is better than death."

Soon their one-eyed host returned. Carefully closing the stone door behind him, he grinned at his guests, his arms full of green seasonings. "This gourmet cooking business is hard work. Yum, yum. I'd kill for another hors d'oeuvre." As Polyphemus reached ravenously toward the back of the sheep pen, Odysseus stepped forward, smiling and holding forth his wineskin.

"Excuse me again for meddling in your menu, pardner, but take a whiff of those appetizers before you chow down. They got a little clumsy and stepped in the wrong place. Kind of turns your stomach, don't it? Here's something to soothe your senses. Try a sip of my homemade wine to tide you over while you're fixin' the main course. It's a fine brew. I guarantee you'll like it!"

115

Polyphemus snatched the wineskin from Odysseus's hand and began to guzzle the powerful liquid. "Mmmm, I have never tasht-ed anything like thish before. Delicioushh! Shhurely it ish nectar from the gods. You know, my father ish a god. Posheidon, god of the shea ... Ha! ... deadbeat dad of the ocean depths."

The Cyclops began to reel. His knees buckled. But he tipped the wineskin for another long swig. "Come, Captain, shquat here beshide me and talk. My nam ish Polyphemush. But you may call me Polly. Whashyer nam? ... Whash *yer* nam? ... Yer nam, yer nam, yer *nam!*"

"My nam? Hmmm ... Oh, yeah, I get your drift. My name. Well, my mama called me *Oudeis*. That's Greek, of course But, you can just call me by my nickname—Nobody."

"Nobody ... Nobody ... never knew a Nobody before. Well, you are my friend, and my guesht, Nobody. And ash my shpe-cial gift to you, Nobody, I will eat you lasht." Polyphemus slurped the last drops of brew from the wineskin. He staggered toward the sheep pen. He belched, his eye closed, his legs fold-ed and—as they say—he hit the hay.

"Sic 'im!" Odysseus yelled to his men. They picked up the sharpened staff and carried it to the fire. When the point was white hot, they raised the great shaft above their heads, backed themselves to the far side of the cave, and then with all the courage and strength they could muster, they ran toward the drunken Cyclops. They drove the smoldering tip into his single eye, twisting the staff like a screw driver.

Polyphemus shrieked and bolted to his feet. He pulled the staff from his forehead. Blood and tissue and mucus poured forth in great abundance. Then with one hand holding his sight-less socket, Polyphemus began to grasp with his other hand for Odysseus. "Where are you, you dishonorable scab of humani-ty? I'll rip out your entrails with my fingernails. Mr. Nobody can't hide from me!"

While the Cyclops bellowed and thrashed about the cave, Odysseus and his men scrambled to hide among the sheep. They lay quietly, scarcely breathing.

Other Cyclopes, sleeping in nearby caves, came running. They called out, "What's the matter, Polyphemus. Is somebody murdering you?"

"Nobody is trying to murder me!"

"Good. If nobody is murdering you, then stop howling and go to sleep."

"No, no. You don't understand. Nobody has blinded me!"

"That's good. Then close your eye and give it a rest."

"No, no. I am in pain! Nobody will suffer for this!"

"You are so wrong. We are suffering already. You were probably having a nightmare. Roll over and go back to sleep, Polyphemus."

Throughout the night, Polyphemus lay in his own blood, writhing and groaning and licking the ooze from his forehead. All the while, Odysseus and his men worked. They tied themselves to the bellies of the largest and shaggiest sheep in the flock. The next morning, Polyphemus crawled to the opening of the cave and pushed aside the boulder, freeing his animals to graze on the hillside. He squatted in the doorway as the sheep ran past him. With his blood-encrusted fingers, he felt the back of every creature, assuring himself that the humans would not escape him.

But of course, Odysseus and his companions did escape the Cyclops, riding to safety while clutching the undersides of the sheep. Once outside, the Greeks untied themselves, dropped to the ground, and ran full speed for their ship.

Meanwhile, the Cyclops rushed to the back of the cave and began to grope around the sheep pen. All he found, of course, was dung. Bellowing in rage, he scurried in blind haste down to the shore, scooped up a large rock and hurled it toward the sound of the departing ship. It landed amidships, crushing five of the crew. Odysseus hollered back, "Goodbye, Polyphemus, you sorry son of a seagod. I've enjoyed about as much of your hospitality as I can stand. If anybody asks who cleaned your plow, tell 'em it was none other than Nobody, soon to be known as Odysseus the Great, top dog in Greece!"

Polyphemus howled toward the sea, "Listen to him, Father Poseidon. Oh woe is me! Prove me your son at last and avenge me!"

From the murky depths of the sea came a voice: "I hear you, I hear you. Now stop blubbering, son, and act like a monster. You start thinking of ways to get even, and I'll put a few hurdles in Odysseus's path. He'll be cursed with storm, shipwreck, and sorcery. And if he ever reaches home, he'll be a beggar and a stranger among his enemies."

And that was exactly what happened to the great Odysseus. He had a mighty hard row to hoe before he beat all the odds, got home, whipped his enemies, and made top dog. Looking back on that encounter with the Cyclops, he later admitted it was like the skunk said when the wind changed: "I should've known it would come back to me."

As for Polyphemus, no one knows for certain what happened to him. Some say he crawled into a cavern deep in the earth and there he still lives. We do know that sometimes the earth shakes and cracks open and swallows human beings alive. And we know that sometimes mountains explode with fire and human beings are roasted to a delicate golden brown. But we don't know why. Maybe, just maybe, it's Polyphemus—still getting even with all us Nobodies.

# A FEW LAST WORDS

As a school librarian and a teacher of storytelling, I cannot resist the professional urge to list a few of my favorite books on Greek mythology. There are a plethora of them on my shelves, and they are all consulted at one time or another. But if you are just beginning a collection of myths, here are my recommendations.

For very young children, these are currently among the best: Marcia Williams' *Greek Myths for Young Children* (Candlewick, 1992), Anne Rockwell's *The Robber Baby* (Greenwillow, 1994), and two modern parallels from Dial Press by Rosemary Wells, *Max and Ruby's First Greek Myth: Pandora* (1993) and *Max and Ruby's Midas* (1995).

Beautifully illustrated books based on individual myths were sparse a decade ago. Publication of such picture books, appropriate for a wide age-range, is now on the rise. The following are among the most visually appealing read-alouds: Leonard Everett Fisher's *Cyclops* (Holiday, 1991), Shirley Climo's *Atalanta's Race* (Clarion, 1995), Kathryn Lasky's *Hercules* (Hyperion, 1997), M. Charlotte Craft's *Cupid and Psyche*

(Morrow, 1996), Gerald McDermott's *Sun Flights* (Four Winds, 1980), Nathaniel Hawthorne's *King Midas and the Golden Touch* (Harcourt, 1987) as retold by Kathryn Hewitt, and *Wings* (Harcourt, 1991) by Jane Yolen.

For upper elementary students and young adult readers, I have found these to be particularly captivating collections that transfer well from page to oral presentation: *D'Aulaire's Book of Greek Myths* (Doubleday, 1962), Geraldine McCaughrean's *Greek Myths* (M.K. McElderry, 1993), Rosemary Sutcliff's account of the *Iliad* in *Black Ships Before Troy* (Delacorte, 1993), and Neil Philip's *The Adventures of Odysseus* (Orchard, 1997).

Adults and secondary students seeking more in-depth and detailed reading will appreciate Donald Richardson's *Greek Mythology for Everyone* (Avenel, 1989), Michael Gibson's *Gods, Men, and Monsters from the Greek Myths* (Schocken's World Mythology Series, 1982), and absolutely anything written by the prolific and provocative Bernard Evslin.

Three books I have found fascinating in their revelation of ancient myths as parallels to the modern world are Paul Fleischman's *Dateline: Troy* (Candlewick, 1996), and Jean Shinoda Bolen's *Goddesses in Every Woman* (Harper, 1984) and *Gods in Every Man* (Harper, 1989).

The standard classics of my youth are as good today as they were a generation ago! Look for these venerable authors: Thomas Bulfinch, Robert Graves, Edith Hamilton, Alfred J. Church, and Padraic Colum.

By far the best modern English translations of Homer's poetic works are by Princeton professor Robert Fagles: *The Iliad* (Viking, 1990) and *The Odyssey* (Viking, 1996). The Homeric tales as well as those of other ancient authors—Hesiod, Euripides, Ovid, Virgil, Sophocles—may be found in Greek or Latin with English translations on opposing pages in the Loeb Classical Library from Harvard University Press.

Two indispensable reference tools that will pique your imagination and supply you with a store of fascinating details about classical mythology are these: *By Jove! Brush Up Your Mythology* (Harper, 1992) by Michael Macrone and *Words from the Myths* (Houghton Mifflin, 1961) by Isaac Asimov.

The mythology of Greece survived for centuries before Gutenberg invented the printing press. To know the stories, one had only to listen to the keepers of the tales—the storytellers. Today, because we no longer need to rely upon the spoken word to know the stories, we forget that they were vividly entertaining vehicles of culture in a prereading era. The best written versions, I believe, remind us once again of the oral power of the ancient myths.

1. Thomas Gray, "Elegy Written in a Country Churchyard," 1750

2. Shakespeare, Sonnet XCIV

3. Shakespeare, Sonnet CXVI

4. Shakespeare, Sonnet LXXIII